THE CON GAME

The Con Game

Hillary Waugh

NEW ENGLISH LIBRARY
TIMES MIRROR

To Larry

First published in Great Britain by Victor Gollancz Ltd. in 1968
Copyright © 1968 by Hillary Waugh

*

THIS SPECIALLY ABRIDGED NEL EDITION MARCH 1970

*

NEL Books are published by
New English Library Limited from Barnard's Inn, Holborn, London E.C.1.
Made and printed in Great Britain by Hunt Barnard & Co. Ltd., Aylesbury, Bucks

45000459 7

PROLOGUE

Mary Fogarty started the record player and the music of Lester Lanin came up loud. "C'mon, everybody," she said. "What are we waiting for?" She went over to where George Demarest, Stan Somers and Carl Randolph were swapping dirty stories.

Mary pulled at Demarest and said, "C'mon, Georgie. Dance with me. Let's get something started here."

Randolph watched them move off, Mary hopping and rocking. "Like an elephant," he muttered to Stan Somers. but Stan wasn't listening. He had spotted Deirdre Demarest standing in a corner alone. His own wife, Jerry, was on the couch with Warren Wilcox and Dixie Randolph, while, across the room, Moira Wilcox was having her ear bent by Dan Fogarty, beside the bottle-loaded table that served as a bar. Stan could make a move to Deirdre, therefore, and it would be perfectly natural. No one would think anything of it. Deirdre was petite, dark-haired and green-eyed, still in her early twenties, and though she never smiled, hardly spoke, and kept herself in the background, she exuded a magnetism that made all men aware of her. And part of her attraction was the sensation she gave that she was equally attracted. It wasn't the way she talked or acted, it was the way she watched men. Watched and waited.

"Well, I might as well get into the act," Stan said to Carl, and he crossed over before somebody else got there first. She saw him coming but neither moved nor looked expectant.

At previous gatherings he had carefully kept his dancing with Deirdre impersonal. One didn't want to get too involved with another man's wife, not when you saw each other all the time, not when your own wife was present, not when Warren Wilcox was already ahead of you in that department. But Jerry had been goading him on of late and this time, when Deirdre moved into his arms and against his body, he kept her close. He was ready to let nature take its course.

Over by the bar, Dan Fogarty poured himself a shot and then, as an afterthought, freshened Moira Wilcox's drink. "So like I was saying," he told her, "it's dog eat dog in my business. You got to cut every corner you can in construction. It ain't like Warren's racket where you sit and wait for the patients to come to you and charge 'em fifty bucks an hour and pack them in standing room. In construction you got a lot of guys trying to underbid you. You got to underbid them to get your share of jobs but that cuts into your profit."

Moira said, "That's very interesting. Remind me to keep an eye on you if we ever hire you to do anything," and she looked over to where Warren was getting up to dance with Dixie Randolph. At least it wasn't with Deirdre this time. And at least it was the Fogartys' house rather than Deirdre's own, which lessened the likelihood that Warren and Deirdre would disappear from the party simultaneously for half an hour. Moira couldn't prove that anything really went on between them, but in her own mind she needed no proof. Warren was dashing and handsome and he knew it and as far as Moira was concerned, all women fell madly in love with him.

Dan put his arm around Moira's waist and hugged her. "Don't you worry. You think I'd cheat a friend?"

Moira said, "No, of course not," without really remembering what he was talking about. She said, "Why don't we dance?" and moved into his arms.

Jerry Somers got off the couch and went to refill her glass. Carl Randolph joined her and said, "You feeling pretty happy tonight?"

She smiled faintly. "It's only seventeen hundred dollars. You're the one who should be on cloud nine. Sixty-three hundred."

"It's too bad Stan couldn't have bought more land. I urged him to."

"Television writers don't have that much extra money. We were lucky we could buy what we did."

"Well don't forget, that seventeen hundred is only the beginning."

"I'm not. That's what makes these affairs bearable." She turned to watch Stan with Deirdre. Jerry shook her head. "Look at her," she said. "A bitch down to her toe-nails."

Carl laughed. "But cute. You want me to cut in?"

"You'd like to, wouldn't you?"

"Just to please you." Randolph went off. Mary Fogarty danced by in George Demarest's arms and said, "Hey, Jerry, get with it."

"I am," Jerry said drily and held up her glass. She did not look at George.

Stan Somers, dispossessed of Deirdre, came to the bar table. Jerry said, "How was she?"

"Deirdre? Nice."

"Ask her to go to bed with you?"

Somers laughed and poured. "Aren't you rushing things a little?"

"I'll bet she would. She's already sleeping with Warren, you know."

"I don't know. But I'd believe it."

"Why?"

"The way she dances—when you let her."

"And that jerk, George, doesn't even notice."

"Maybe he only pretends he doesn't. Maybe Warren bought a big insurance policy from him."

"That would be George. But one of these days you ought to take her up on it, sweetie. She's probably hot stuff in bed."

Stan shook his head and eyed her. "The way you harp on my going to bed with her, I think you really wouldn't mind."

Jerry patted his arm and smiled. "Just so long as you don't make it a habit."

One song ended and another started. Dixie Randolph and Warren Wilcox came over and Dixie said, "Break it up, you two. Husbands and wives together are illegal." She took Stan away for a dance and Warren said to Jerry, "At last. You and I alone."

"In a crowd." She saw Wilcox's eyes dart momentarily at Deirdre and said when she moved into his arms, "Does she do it on her back or on her side or on her stomach?"

"Does who do what?"

"Skip it. What about Moira? Does she give you a hard time?"

Wilcox looked properly puzzled. "You've lost me. Does Moira give me a hard time about what?"

"Deirdre, of course."

"Deirdre?"

"Deirdre. You and Deirdre. Come on, Warren. Stop pretending."

He laughed. "That's your imagination. You're as bad as Moira yourself."

"Then she does give you a hard time about her."

"Moira gives me a hard time about every woman I look at. Right now she's measuring us and wondering what we mean to each other."

"Who says? You aren't even looking at her."

"I don't have to look. I've been married to her for eighteen years and I'm a psychiatrist. Remember? I know her inside out."

"Lie down on my couch and I will."

Jerry smiled up at him. "Do you know me inside out?"

7

"No thanks. I might show up in that book you're writing."

He laughed. "I thought you were going to say something else."

"About the lying down part?"

"I thought your mind would work along those lines."

"Oh. You think you *do* know me then. That reminds me. About that couch business. Are you getting the material for your book firsthand or secondhand?"

He laughed again. "You see? That *is* where your mind is oriented."

"And where is your mind oriented? On Deidre?"

"You're sounding like Moira again. Let me explain that Deirdre is pretty and appealing—"

"And such a conversationalist, too."

"Oh, she talks."

"But not in public. I've hardly ever heard her open her mouth."

"She's ill at ease around women. She doesn't know how to handle herself."

"They don't respond to her big eyes and sex appeal. I wonder if she and George ever talk. Or do they spend all their time in bed?"

"You'd know better than I, I expect."

She looked up at him. "Maybe not better. Maybe only as well."

Dan Fogarty stopped the record player and called out, "O.K., let's have a toast." He raised a glass with an inch of liquor in it. "It may be the twenty-fifth of January," he said, "but for us it's New Year's Eve. So here's to 1966, the best year yet. And here's to Carl Randolph, the best damned real estate agent in the whole damned state—in the whole damned country. And here's to us, the greatest bunch of guys and gals who ever came down the pike. We're all pals forever!"

8

1

Chief of Police Fred C. Fellows sat down at his desk and opened his Thermos. The eight o'clock shift had been dispatched to its duties and now he poured a cup of black coffee and settled down to his own business of looking over reports. Then Detective Lieutenant Sidney Wilks opened the door. "You've got a customer, Fred, who says he wants to see the chief. Nothing else will do." Fellows smiled faintly and got to his feet.

Outside, in the large main room, was a stocky sandy-haired man wearing slacks and an open blue sport shirt. Fellows, looking him over, guessed his age as mid-forties, height five ten, weight better than two hundred.

"I'm the chief." Fellows said. "You wanted to see me?"

"Yeah, I do. My name's Dan Fogarty and I own a construction company. The Fogarty Construction Company. Maybe you know it?"

"I know of it. What can we do for you, Mr. Fogarty?"

"I want you to arrest a man."

Wilks got into the chair behind the main desk and Fellows leaned an arm on its top. "Arrest what man?"

"A guy by the name of George Demarest. That's who."

"What's the complaint?"

"He cheated me out of nine thousand dollars. I guess that ought to be complaint enough."

"It sounds like enough. How did he cheat you?"

Fogarty gestured. "This guy, this Demarest, is an insurance agent, see?"

"Oh?" Fellows frowned. "That George Demarest?"

"You know him?"

"Only that he's got an agency in town."

"Yeah," Fogarty went on, "well here's what happened. I'm taking out a big policy with this guy. And the first payment is nine thousand dollars. Well, I give him the nine thousand. But I don't have no insurance policy."

"Did you ask him about it?"

Fogarty's voice came up. "How can I ask him about it? He's not in town any more. He took my nine thousand and scrammed."

Fellows was soothing. "Now let's go easy, Mr. Fogarty. If I'm not mistaken, Demarest has had an insurance agency in Stockford for quite a few years. I don't think he'd be trying a thing like that."

"Then suppose you tell me where he went and where's my nine thousand dollars!"

"All right. First off, are you sure he's left town?"

"Am I sure? You think I haven't been to his house half a dozen times? You think I haven't called his office till I'm blue in the face? You think I don't know a car's missing outta his garage?" He jabbed his finger at the chief. "You wantta know the proof? I'll tell you the proof. I checked with his dairy and I got it from them that he canceled his milk deliveries the day after I give him the money."

Fellows shrugged. "When was all this?"

"Back on Wednesday, August twenty-fourth. That's when I give him the money. It was Friday morning when the milkman found the note. That means Demarest left town the day after I paid him!"

Fellows looked at Wilks and Wilks spread his hands. "A vacation? Maybe he—"

Fogarty's voice was a squeal. "A vacation on my nine thousand bucks. That's what kind of a vacation it is." He turned to Fellows. "I want you to arrest him and get me back my nine thousand bucks!"

"All right, Mr. Fogarty, I know you're excited, but let's not be hasty about this. Think about it for a minute. Mr. Demarest would hardly run off with your money. It wouldn't be worth it to him."

"Talk, talk. Who says he wouldn't? Nine thousand bucks isn't chickenfeed in anybody's language."

Fellows looked at Wilks and got out a notebook. "Where does George Demarest live?"

"Twenty-six Sleetwood Road. Corner of Harris."

"In the Crestwood section?" Fellows wrote and looked up. "He own his own house?"

"I don't know. I think so."

"And you said a car is missing? Did he have more than one?"

"Yeah. The station wagon's still there."

Fellows was soothing. "What probably happened is he turned your money over to the insurance company he represents and then went on vacation. And, due to some delay—remember it takes time to process a large policy—maybe the application got lost, maybe your policy got held up in the mail. Why don't you—"

"Like hell the policy got lost in the mail. There isn't any policy. You think I didn't check with the insurance company? They never got word of any such policy. He didn't hand any money over to them, he kept it himself and left town with it."

"Has you check been cashed? Have you got your bank statements yet?"

"Yes and yes. He cashed it the day I give it to him. August twenty-fourth. And he beat it out of town the next day. When I give him the money he told me I'd have the policy the next day. Now if he told me that and the insurance company says they never heard of the policy, what're you gonna believe—that the insurance company's crooked or that he's crooked?"

Fellows smiled. "I guess you've got me there. And you're sure he never mentioned anything to you about going away?"

"The hell he did. He made me believe he was going to stay put."

"All right, Mr. Fogarty, we'll look into it." He took down Fogarty's address which was on May Street in the middle-class development by Indian River, saw him to the outside steps, gave him further reassurance and closed the door after him.

He came back shaking his head and smiled at Wilks. "Well, Sid, what do you make of that one?"

"A little hysterical, our Mr. Fogarty."

"But it doesn't make any sense. Demarest's had an agency here for—it must be ten years. He's got a house up in Crestwood. That's a better section than Fogarty lives in. He's not going to throw all that over for any nine thousand dollars. My guess is Fogarty's leaping to wrong conclusions and the whole thing will be cleared up as soon as Demarest gets back."

"Which will be when?"

"Why don't you go find out?"

2

Sidney Wilks pulled up in front of 26 Sleetwood Road, shut off the motor and surveyed the scene. The Demarest home was a rancher in the $25,000 class, a little large for the lot, but so were all the others. There was a driveway on the left to a two-car garage and connecting breezeway in back, a couple

11

of fledgling trees in the small lawn in front, and shielding shrubbery along the property line of the next house and down the sidewalk on Harris Street. Curtains were drawn at all the windows, the lawn needed mowing and the mailbox was full, with additional letters and magazines lying on the steps in front of the door.

Wilks bit off some chewing tobacco and sat for a bit getting the feel of the area, trying to sense what it was like living there, what kind of people sought out $25,000 homes on 70' x 150' lots. When the mailman made his deposit on the Demarest steps. Wilks slipped out and circled the car. "Say," he said as the mailman came back, "you know the people who live here?"

The mailman paused and shrugged. "Name's Demarest. That's as far as I go."

"They away?"

"Seem to be. Vacation probably."

"They haven't moved or anything?"

"Not so far as the post office knows."

The man went on and Wilks walked up to the door. He pushed the bell and heard it ring inside. He opened the screen and tried the inside knob. He checked some of the mail for postmarks. A couple of bills were dated *Aug 24.* That went with Fogarty's story.

Wilks crossed the street then to where an old man, on his knees, was excising crabgrass with a buttonhook knife, using a peach basket for the weedings.

"Hot work," Wilks said.

The man looked up. "Good for what ails you," he said. "Gets the poisons out of your system." He gazed at his grass with pride.

"I'm looking for the Demarests," Wilks motioned with his thumb. "People across the street."

"I noticed."

"They don't seem to be home."

"I expect he works. I'm retired."

"You know them well?"

"I've seen them a few times."

"But you don't know them?"

"Think he's in insurance. Don't know more about him than that."

"You wouldn't know where they went?"

"I didn't know they went anywhere."

"Do you remember the last time you saw them?"

The man sat back on his knees and took out a large handkerchief to wipe his face. "Nope. Can't say I do. Once in a while a car goes out or comes in. Can't say I pay much attention."

Wilks thanked the man and recrossed the street, this time going up the drive for a look at the back. There was a small square stoop with a milk box on it and a half-empty can of insect spray. Window shades were drawn there too and the back door was as tightly locked as the front.

Wilks went out the short breezeway to the side door of the garage. Inside, a dirty blue station wagon occupied the nearer space. The other space was empty and both overhead doors were closed. Wilks stepped back out and wandered at random around the yard. It was grass and dirt with a couple of large trees hampering each other's struggle for sunlight. The screening bushes were overgrown from lack of pruning, the grass was dry and brown from the drought and thin from a life in the shade. George Demarest didn't covet lush lawns like his neighbor across the street, nor did he fancy flowers. Though there was ample space, there were no gardens. There never had been any gardens. There was only a picnic table and two benches, four lawn chairs and a metal stand, none of which appeared to have been recently used.

If the property told a little about the Demarests it said nothing about where they went and Wilks tried the house next door, cutting through one of the gaps between bushes at the back. The layout there was much the same as the Demarests' except there were no trees in the yard and there was a garden by the detached garage. Lawn furniture and a picnic and barbecue setup were in evidence and, though weathered, were better kept up.

A graying woman in mid-forties answered the door on Wilks' first ring and said, "Sorry, but we're not interested."

"I'm not selling anything, ma'am. I'm looking for the Demarests."

"Oh." She gestured. "That's their house. Next door."

"They seem to be away. I was wondering if you might know where they went."

"I'm sorry. We've been away ourselves. Only got back Labor Day. We haven't seen the Demarests."

"Do you know them?"

"Not well. My husband and George Demarest chat now and then by the bushes. We're friendly but not intimate."

"But you haven't seen them since you got back?"

"No. I expect they've gone on vacation."

"Did they mention they were going on vacation?"

The woman said, "We've been away all summer. My husband teaches. He was doing research in Oxford. I'm

13

afraid we're a little out of touch."

"They have other friends or relatives? Someone who might know where they went?"

"I really don't know anything about their relatives. They do have some friends. People come to visit them and they go out —I suppose to see people—but I don't know who they are."

A car pulled into the drive and the woman said, "Here's my husband. Perhaps he can help you."

A man with shaggy brown hair, a rumpled suit and an open, relaxed face, got out with a bag of groceries and said, "Sorry, Pet, no frozen mashed potatoes."

She said, "I thought this was the land of heat-and-serve. We might as well be back in England. This is Mr.—ah—I don't know his name. He's looking for the Demarests."

"Oh, and here I thought I was coming home at just the wrong time." He held out a hand to Wilks. "Herrick's the name. Bob Herrick."

Wilks introduced himself as a detective lieutenant. Herrick said, "Oh? Police?" and raised an eyebrow. "Have they done something they shouldn't?"

Wilks said, "We just want to get in touch with them."

"Can't help you there," Herrick answered. "We haven't seen them since June."

"Can you tell me anything about him? Relatives, friends, anyone who might know where they've gone?"

" 'Fraid I don't know anything about that. I'm afraid, Lieutenant, we're not the right place for information. Not about them, anyway."

"Mrs. Herrick tells me you and Demarest have had chats together."

"Yes, but I really don't know anything about George Demarest. He's in the insurance business. He's young—say thirty-five. His wife is very very young. Early twenties, mid-twenties, somewhere around there. You agree, Pet? He's a Babbitt type, I suppose, a prosaic individual." He spread his hands. "I think that's about it."

"Was he a successful insurance agent? Was he pretty well heeled?"

"Oh, I suppose so. But of course that's a prejudiced opinion. I tend to think everybody in business is enormously success-ful. Otherwise I can't imagine why they'd be in business. I like to think it's only we teachers who have to worry these days about how to keep the wolf from the door. Regarding his wife, I think he is the jealous type but then, that's another prejudiced opinion. If I were married to a young and beauti-ful thing like her, I wouldn't let her out of my sight. They

14

didn't seem to entertain a great deal or go out much. Of course there are any number of other possible explanations for that."

"There are, but you like that one."

"Well, I do and I don't quite know why."

"I can tell you why," his wife said. "It was the way she looked at you. What I mean is that she had a way of looking at all men. You might call it an indiscriminate look."

Wilks said, "Are you suggesting they didn't get along?"

"Oh," she answered, "they fought. You could hear them."

"Know about what?"

Herrick said, "No, and it wasn't that often. But now and then they'd have a Donnybrook. Nothing physical though. He never beat her so far as I know."

"What I really want to know is where they went."

Herrick laughed. "Which brings us full circle. We've already said we don't know where they went. Shall we start around again?"

Wilks shook his head. "Only if you can give me an idea why they might go away. I mean other than vacation."

Neither of them could and Wilks took his leave.

3

Wilks relieved Chernoff at the desk when he came back at half-past ten. He uncased the portable typewriter and pecked out a report and was editing it when Fellows returned from investigating a case of vandalism at a construction site.

"You find out anything about what's-his-name?"

"Demarest? Only that nobody's seen him for a couple of weeks. The house is locked, shades drawn, mail piling up. I checked his office on the way back. That's locked too."

"Mail piling up? What kind of mail?"

"Bills, circulars, magazines, junk stuff. No personal letters, at least with a return address on them."

Fellows rubbed his chin. "They cancel milk deliveries but don't ask that the mail be held?"

"Which is what people would probably do if they weren't going to be away very long."

"Or if they were going to be away longer and forgot."

"And either way it spells vacation. At least to me."

"To me too, except for that nine thousand dollars. I don't get that at all."

"Probably an oversight or a slip-up somewhere."

"*Probably*. And *probably* it's a vacation. But we don't know either of those things for sure. You get the names of friends or relatives—people he might tell his plans to?"

"Not yet. I rang every doorbell in the neighborhood but nobody, outside of the people next door, knows anything more than what he looks like."

Fellows picked up Wilks' report and read it through rapidly. "Fight with his wife, huh?"

"So the man says."

"And jealous."

"And the wife is beautiful and has a wandering eye. Or so says a couple who probably wouldn't know a wandering eye if they saw one."

Fellows put the report aside and rubbed his chin. "Nobody in the neighborhood saw them leave, is that right?"

"That's right."

"And he didn't tell them he was going on a vacation and nobody noticed anything that might make them think he was— you know, shopping expeditions, hanging out clothes and all?"

"The only people who could have seen them hang out clothes were away all summer. What are you thinking about— that they never left?"

Fellows frowned. "The possibility strikes me."

"You think they dropped dead in the house, committed suicide, or were murdered?"

"Well, he's supposed to have had a check for nine thousand dollars. People have been robbed and killed for less."

"They went away, Fred. One of their cars is gone."

"One is gone if they had two. How do we know they had two?"

"Fogarty said—"

"That's right. And Fogarty also says Demarest stole money from him, which doesn't make any sense. I don't put a great deal of faith in what Mr. Fogarty says."

"Then you think the Demarests might have been robbed and killed?"

"No. I think they went away. But there's something funny about the whole thing and I'm not going to feel easy until I know for sure. I want to see the inside of their house, Sid. If they're there, it's time we found out. If they aren't, there might be something there that'll tell us where they went."

Wilks got up. "O.K., let's take a look."

"Slow it down a little. Call Chernoff in while I go upstairs

16

and see if Cobbit Reed's around. Just in case there's more to this than we think, I'd like a search warrant in my hand to make it all nice and legal."

They parked in the drive in front of the garage and Fellows made no immediate effort to enter the house. Instead he wandered over the grass and took a look at the picnic table and outdoor furniture. Then he walked over to the side garage door and went in. Wilks followed and when Fellows looked thoughtfully at the dirty five-year-old station wagon and opened the door to lean inside, he said, "You looking for anything special?"

"Sixty-eight thousand miles," Fellows said, backing out and slamming the door. "No, I'm just trying to get a feel of the place."

"You won't find any bodies out here. I already looked."

"Sid, you don't enjoy anticipation." He wandered over to a pair of worn tires leaning against the back wall of the empty stall, bent and read the tire sizes and said, "They probably do have two cars. These wouldn't fit the station wagon."

"When did you get to be an expert on tire sizes?"

"This morning. I was studying some sheets I've got with tire treads, sizes, and what goes on what car. The tread pattern we found at the site fits a tire that will go on Fords and you know the six teenagers from Pittsfield Daniels stopped last night for whooping and hollering around town? They were in a Ford."

"Manny knows about that?"

"Yeah. I figured there might be a connection." Fellows paused and looked over a small collection of tools standing in a corner. There was a powered reel mower, a new pointed shovel crusted with dirt, a rake with leaves caught on it whose rustiness indicated it had been purchased a long time ago but whose polished handle and fresh-looking paint indicated it had hardly been used, a similar, rusty but little-used ax, and a bamboo rake with a number of broken prongs. Fellows picked up the ax and examined the blade, running a finger along its sharp cutting edge. Wilks said, "No blood?"

"No blood." Fellows picked up a peach basket full of waste rags, set it down and looked at the scattering of cans containing oil, dried paint brushes and weed killer. Then he went out again.

"You getting much of a feel?" Wilks asked when Fellows mounted the stoop, paused to observe the insect spray can and open the empty milk box.

"I'd guess Mr. Demarest isn't much on household chores.

Doesn't use his tools much, doesn't take care of his paint brushes. Now let's see what kind of a lock we've got here."

It took a minute to identify the lock and pick the proper key from the large ring the chief took from his pocket. He fitted the key in the slot, opened the door and pushed it wide.

The breakfast nook was beside the door. Beyond, a separating counter bounded the sink, stove and icebox area. Fellows viewed the scene from the doorway for a moment and then stepped inside. He sniffed the stale air, observed that the table and counters were clean, and went to open the cupboards. China and glasses were neatly stacked.

Wilks said, "I don't smell any bodies." He opened the refrigerator and made a face. "But I can smell that all right."

"Let's see." Fellows moved in for a look. The refrigerator was well-stocked with food but the perishables were odorous and the milk had curdled.

They went through the dining room into the living room. Both were reasonably neat except for cobwebs in the corners near the ceiling and two unemptied ashtrays on the coffee table. There were eight butts in them, three with lipstick.

Fellows observed them without touching and without comment. He picked up and thumbed through several magazines in a rack by one of the chairs and moved into Demarest's study. No papers strewed the desk-top, nothing was in the wastebasket, the file cabinet was closed and locked.

The adjoining bath was in order and so was the guest room.

They went into the master bedroom and Wilks, pausing to view it from the doorway, said, "Well, at least she didn't forget to make the bed."

Fellows opened one of the closets. Two summer dresses and half a dozen empty hangers hung inside. On the floor four pairs of shoes were scattered. He opened the other, found three pairs of men's shoes and one wrinkled Madras jacket. "I'd have to guess they own more clothes than this," he said.

Wilks, going through bureau drawers, said, "And more than they've got here. A couple of pairs of socks and shorts, no shirts for George. Only a few underthings for the wife."

Fellows checked the bathroom, found two toothbrushes in the rack and the usual items in the medicine cabinet.

They tried the cellar last. Winter clothes were stored in a closet by the furnace in mothproof bags. The only other item of note was a toolbox which looked unused. "No suitcases," Wilks said. "Most of the summer clothes gone. What would you guess? A resort?"

Fellows withdrew a packet of chewing tobacco from his shirt pocket and bit off a piece. "Probably," he said. "I don't see anything offhand to tell me different. A small party the night before they left, apparently. Three different brands of cigarettes in the ashtrays, two different shades of lipstick on two different kinds of butts."

They headed for the stairs and Wilks said, "So now what do you propose to do? Track him down and demand Fogarty's nine thousand dollars?"

"That's the clinker," Fellows said. "Throw in the car, all those winter clothes, the furniture, and you've got more than nine thousand dollars worth of stuff left behind. Wherever they went, they're coming back. They're not running off with his money."

"He thinks they are."

"He tells us he thinks they are."

"Then you don't believe him?"

"Dammit, Sid, that story doesn't fit what we find. No, I don't believe him."

They locked up the house and went back to the car. When the chief started up, Wilks said, "Do you think Fogarty's lying to us outright, or do you think he's just made a mistake?"

"That's what I want to know. Let's try the banks on our way back."

The teller in the first bank they stopped at, the Stockford Trust Company, looked nervously at the big-framed chief of police. He breathed more easily when Fellows made his simple request. Did Dan Fogarty have his checking account at that bank? The teller was glad to go through the records. Yes, yes. Mr. Fogarty did have an account.

Fellows said, "I'd like to know about a check he's supposed to have drawn for nine thousand dollars last month. I'd like to know when it was made out, when it was cashed and by who."

It took the teller fifteen minutes and he returned to the window perspiring. "I'm very sorry for the delay," he said. "But I've checked and rechecked. Nobody's tried to cash a check signed by Mr. Fogarty for nine thousand dollars, either last month or any other month I can find. And they couldn't do it if they tried. Mr. Fogarty doesn't have enough money in his account to cover it."

4

Fellows' dinner that Thursday evening was almost like old times. True, his daughter Shirley was teaching in Maine for the second year, but Larry and his bride of nine months, Denise, were eating with them and it made the table full again. Soon, however—all too soon—only he and Cessie would be sitting down to evening meals. Katie was twenty now, starting her junior year in teachers' college and Peter, at seventeen, was in his last year at Stockford High. What would Cessie do with herself with no children to manage? What would they talk about when offspring no longer posed problems? They did talk of other things, he knew, but right then he couldn't think what they were. But he didn't want to think. He wanted to enjoy his family while he could.

It didn't last long. Dessert was no sooner over than Larry glanced at his watch and said, "Hey, Denise and I want to catch a show. We're going to have to go. Gee, that was a good dinner, Mom."

"I guess you'd better," Fellows said and smiled. He saw them out the door and returned to where Cessie and Katie were clearing the table. Cessie said, "I like Denise. She's a nice girl."

"Yeah. Do you think she's pregnant?"

Cessie stopped and looked at him. "Whatever gave you that idea?"

"I'm just wondering."

"You don't sound very happy at the propect. Don't you want to be a grandfather?"

"I don't know. You see that new car Larry's bought? I don't know how he can manage the payments on what he makes."

"I'm sure they can or he wouldn't have bought it."

"With both of them working, yes. But if she should have a baby and have to give up her job and he'd have all that expense besides. I didn't buy a new car until—"

"Oh, now, Fred." She paused and watched him pin his badge back on his shirt. "Are you going out?"

"I'm picking up Sid at eight o'clock. We have a little job to do."

Wilks came out of his house as Fellows pulled up in front. It was a short drive and they pulled up in front of a house on May Street near the river. Fellows said, "Can you make out the number?"

"Yeah. This is the place."

They got out and went up the walk together, shoulder to shoulder, both men so broad each had a foot on the grass. Fellows rang the bell and they didn't talk now and they didn't smile. This was business.

Dan Fogarty was the one who answered. He turned on the outside light, opened the door and found himself looking into two grim faces. He opened the screen door for them. "You find that guy already? You got my money back?"

They went into the living room where Mrs. Fogarty, plump and plain, with unnaturally red hair, looked up from the television and came to her feet.

Fellows said, "May we speak to your husband alone, Mrs. Fogarty?"

"Hey, that's all right," Fogarty said. "She knows all about it. You can talk in front of her."

"You want that?"

"Sure." Fogarty began to notice that the police didn't seem the bearers of good news. "Why? What's it all about?"

"That's what we're here to find out."

"Huh? I don't get you." Fogarty sank slowly into his chair like a balloon deflating. "What's the matter?"

"Mr. Fogarty," Fellows said in a cold voice, "do you know the penalties for making false accusations, for lying to the police?"

"Lying to the police?" Fogarty came half out of the chair again.

"Sit down, Fogarty. I don't know what grievance you may have against George Demarest, but when you spread false rumors against him you're in serious trouble. And when you come to the police with them you're in worse trouble."

Mary Fogarty's mouth opened and she sat too. Her husband sputtered, "What are you talking about? I wasn't lying. He stole nine thousand bucks off me!"

"Fogarty, I have a warrant for your arrest in my pocket. For making false statements to the police. I don't know what Mr. Demarest may want to do to you, but *I* can do plenty. What I do depends on what you have to say for yourself."

Fogarty and his wife both turned white. Fogarty said, "Listen, what're you talking about? I'm not trying to con you. I gave George Demarest nine thousand dollars and he ran away with it."

Fellows said impatiently, "I don't want to hear that story again. The Demarests went away but they didn't take nine

21

thousand dollars of your money with them because you never paid them any nine thousand. We've been to your bank. There's no check and you know it."

"I didn't pay him by check, I paid him cash."

"You told me check."

"If I did, I made a mistake. I meant to say cash."

"You meant to say 'check' and you claimed the check had been cashed. Now don't try to make me believe you paid him nine thousand dollars in cash. Where's your receipt?"

Fogarty gulped and swallowed. "I don't have one. I lost it. I don't know where it is."

Fellows snorted. "You lost it! All right, where'd you get the cash?"

"I sold some stock. I took the rest out of my bank account."

"How much did you take out of the bank?"

"Seventy-three hundred."

"Let me see your bankbook."

"Yeah, sure." Fogarty started to rise and slumped suddenly back. He rubbed a hand over his face. "Well, I didn't take it all out at once. It was a thousand here, five hundred there. I took it out a little at a time."

"Meaning you can't prove you ever gave him anything."

"Yeah," Fogarty admitted sourly, "that's right." He looked up and waved a hand. "But he took it even if I can't prove it. That's why I went to you. *You're* supposed to prove it."

Fellows looked him over coldly. "Mr. Fogarty, you're a successful businessman. You're no little old lady waiting to be duped by a smart con man. You know what the wicked world is all about."

"Yeah. Sure I do."

"So don't try to tell me you collected nine thousand in cash, a little at a time, to pay for an insurance policy and gave it to the man without even a receipt."

His wife said, "What'd you tell 'em insurance for? Whyn't you tell 'em the truth?"

He wheeled on her. "Shut your mouth."

"What're you trying to be loyal to them for? They all got together and took you for nine thousand dollars and you're going to protect them? Well, I'll tell if you won't."

"They got taken too, you cluck. So shut your face."

Fellows turned to her. "Who's they?"

"Randolph, Somers and Wilcox," she shouted. "Them and their snotty wives. Them and Demarest."

Fellows said, "Randolph, Somers and Wilcox? Who are they?"

She snorted loudly. "Carl Randolph, the big-shot real estate

22

agent. Randolph Real Estate. And his big-shot cousin, Stan Somers, who writes for television. And Warren Wilcox, the big-shot psychiatrist. Big-shots, my eye. Big crooks."

Fogarty said, "They don't want me blabbing. I wouldn't've said a word except the old lady was on my back."

"Yeah," she came back, her voice rising. "When somebody cheats you out of nine thousand bucks, you can damned well bet I'm not going to take that lying down."

Fellows broke in. "All right, we've got some names. Now we want the picture. What's it all about?"

Fogarty said, "There's no picture. I'm withdrawing my complaint."

"You're not withdrawing anything, mister. Now I want the whole story, including why you're doing this about-face. If you don't want to tell it to me here, we'll take you downtown. And if you don't talk there, we'll put you in a cell and come back and talk to your wife. And if she won't talk, then we'll take it up with Randolph and the rest of them."

"Well, goddammit," Fogarty said, "there's nothing to tell. Demarest fed us a line of crap and we all bit. Then he collected himself forty-six thousand dollars and took off."

"Sixty thousand," said his wife.

"Forty-five thousand, nine hundred and fifty dollars," Fogarty said back. "The other fourteen thousand fifty was his own."

"I don't care how you juggle the figures, he walked out with sixty thousand dollars. Him and that minx he was married to."

"Aah, she didn't have nothing to do with it."

Fellows said, "Cut the bickering. Do you want to talk or do you want to get locked up?"

Fogarty gestured. "I got nothing to hide. I'd've told you the whole thing in the first place, 'cepting the rest of the guys didn't want me to. Make a deal with you. I talk and you keep quiet. Don't let on I mentioned their names."

"No deal. I'm going to be talking to all of them whether you talk or not. I don't know what's going on but I'm going to find out. And I mean *I'm going to find out.*"

5

"This time I'm telling you the honest-to-God truth," Fogarty said, sounding earnest. "I wouldda told you before but the others, they wanted it quiet. But I'm not about to sit still and be robbed. So all I was trying to do was get my dough back without dragging them in. O.K., so now you don't give me no choice. Just don't let on. O.K.?"

"Just you tell us the honest-to-God truth," Fellows snapped.

"I am. I'm trying to. Ya see, I got some property up off Long Mountain Road near Vesper. Twenty-eight acres of woods. Bought it a year and a half ago on speculation. I figured if I could someday raise the dough to develop it, I could clean up. Even if I couldn't, it's a good buy, what with real estate going up. So I got some extra dough, I figured I'd put it in land and see what I could do for myself, O.K.?"

"O.K."

"So then, last fall, Persall Brothers make me an offer for it. You know Persall Brothers? They're a big out-of-state developer. They buy up large tracts, build up whole communities and sell them off.

"They want my twenty-eight acres and offer seven hundred an acre. I only paid five hundred six months before. That's not a bad profit for six months, especially since I can't see myself doing anything with the land in the foreseeable future. On the other hand, I'm no damned fool. I can figure just as well as you that they want my twenty-eight as part of a bigger parcel and if I hold out, they're going to go higher.

"So next thing I know, I get a phone call from this Carleton Randolph, the real estate guy. House on Cobblers Lane and all that. He's loaded. And he asks if I've had an offer and asks me not to make any deals yet but meet with him at his house on a certain night.

"I don't know what he's up to, see? Except that he can't be going to bid against Persall and try to develop the land himself. He may be big in Stockford but he doesn't have that kind of dough. I figure more likely he thinks I've got a key piece and he's going to try to get it from me before Persall does and then make them pay through the nose. So that's O.K. with me. Let me get them bidding against each other and I'm going to come up roses.

"Well, I go to his house and it turns out I'm not the only

one showing up. There's this guy, Stan Somers, who writes for television and who, it turns out, is a cousin of Randolph's. And there's Warren Wilcox, the psychiatrist, and there's George Demarest, who's in insurance. That's five of us, counting Randolph, see? And it's a funny combination. A real estate guy, a television writer, a psychiatrist, an insurance agent and me, a contractor. Well, come to find out, the five of us happen to own all the land that Persall wants to buy. A big, fat, hundred and eighty-eight acres. The whole woods.

"So Randolph makes his pitch. He thinks Persall will go very high for the land and if we band together and not make separate deals, we can all get the maximum price. He claims in unity there is strength and we'll all do better together than any of us could do dealing with Persall alone. So he wants us to put him in charge of negotiations—subject to our approval, of course."

Fellows said, "What would he get out of it?"

"A big fat profit. Out of that hundred and eighty-eight acres, Carl owns sixty-three. He bought it last year, like me, but instead of planning to build on it, he planned to subdivide it into lots and sell them off at a profit. But, with Persall interested, he can make a real killing and he wants to make it as big a killing as he can. He wants to charge them all the traffic will bear. But he figures he can't hold out for the maximum unless we do too, see?

"Well, Demarest, he's not much interested. He's got forty-four acres he bought back in '62 when the price was only three hundred and to him that seven hundred Persall is offering looks good. He wants to grab it when he can. As for me, I don't need nobody else doing my dickering for me. I figure I could hold out and get a thousand and I'd be a fool not to take it.

"So we're not sold but we're willing to listen if Randolph's got something to tell us. So he says what he really thinks is going on is that the state is planning to put a highway through and the Persall people know about it and that's why they want the land. Randolph's guess is that they wouldn't build a flock of houses out in no-man's land unless there was going to be an easy way for the owners to get where it counts. And it's a cinch the roads we got around there now aren't it.

"Well, then Demarest says that his company's offices are in Hartford and he has a lot of contacts there and he knows a guy connected with the highway commission and he could feel him out and see if that's the story. Because, as Randolph says, if there's going to be a highway, then that land is going sky high.

"So we all agree we'll stall Persall for a bit and have another meeting. We do. We have one at Demarest's house a few days later and he's got it from the horse's mouth that a thruway is going near our land. Well, we hear that and we start thinking in big figures. Persall's going to have to pay to get our land now. We all agree we're in it together, all the way, and Carl will represent us. And that's what we tell the Persall guys the next time they come nosing around.

"So we got a combine going. It's a real club. We hold dinner parties every Tuesday—different person's house—and Randolph gives us the latest word. First it's a thousand Persall's offering, and we laugh. Then it gets up to twelve hundred and then fifteen. Carl laughs in their faces. He tells them he knows about the highway and he wants three thousand. Of course that's way out of line but it's a bargaining point."

Fellows said, "O.K., I get the idea. What happened?"

"All right, what finally happened was that Persall offered two thousand and we took it. Not an outright sale, of course, but a year's option to buy at two thousand, five percent down to hold the option. So the checks come in and on January twenty-fifth we have a big celebration at my house and Carl passes out the option checks. Sixty-three hundred for himself, forty-four hundred for Demarest, thirty-six for Wilcox, twenty-eight for me, and seventeen hundred for Stan Somers. We're pretty happy, see? You better believe we were."

Fellows said patiently, "I'm still waiting to hear about sixty thousand dollars you claim Demarest ran off with."

"Yeah." Fogarty's face turned sour. "That day we got the option checks, that was the high point. After that is was nothing but trouble. All trouble."

"That's what I want to hear about."

"I'm telling you! First of all, the group kind of breaks up. We're all supposed to be pals, but once we get the deal set, there aren't so many meetings any more."

"Anyway, a couple of months go by with us hardly seeing each other, but then we begin to wonder about the damned highway and when Persall's coming through with the rest of the dough. Sure we get to keep the five percent if they don't exercise the option but what the hell's a hundred bucks an acre? We want the other nineteen hundred.

"So Demarest says he'll talk to his friends in Hartford and find out about the damned highway and the next thing we know, what he's found out is there's an alternate route the highway might take. It's all a question of which one is best from the standpoint of cost and population development and things like that.

"Well, we aren't too worried at first. We figure Persall must have inside info or inside influence and it would end up going our way. But then we come to find out that Persall Brothers not only has an option on our land, they've got an option on a two hundred and twenty-one acre tract along the *other* route the highway might go. So it doesn't mean a thing to them which one the highway department picks. They're covered, see? In fact, it's to their advantage to have it go the other way because they've got that land for three quarters the price of ours. Fourteen hundred and fifty dollars an acre to be exact. So whatever influence they've got, they'd be using to swing the road the other way."

Fogarty slapped his knees. "Well, we're feeling pretty sunk. We figure with Persall on the other side of the fence, we're out in the cold. So then Stan Somers says he doesn't see how Persall could influence the highway department anyway and he thinks we've got an even chance. Well, Somers isn't so smart about those things. I know enough about construction and Demarest knows enough about Hartford politics to let Somers know it's not the highway department you're talking about. They've got to have test borings made, they've got to hire firms to figure the number of bridges, cost of condemning land, and all of those things plus feeding stuff into computers to figure population trends. They're going to have to get reports on all those things in order to figure costs and which is the best way. And if you know the right people to see, and you grease the right palms, why the reports that the highway commission gets will say what you want them to say.

"Well, I guess the idea hits us all about the same time. Maybe we can find out who you talk to and who you pay off to get the reports to say what *we* want. So Demarest looks into that and we're holding these weekly meetings again, see? And Demarest gets a couple of people down from Hartford. One had something to do with geology and there was another guy who was an engineer and they were connected with firms that would be doing this study work for the highway department. And they didn't commit themselves or anything but they sounded like we could do business with them.

"Well, there were three or four of those guys, but it's like groping in the dark. You don't know how many guys you're going to have to buy. You don't know which reports are going to carry what weight with the highway commission.

"So then one night Demarest shows up with a guy named Hal. No last name. We were to call him 'Hal.' Well, it turns out this Hal is an agent for a guy he doesn't identify. He just calls him the Big Boy. And he says the Big Boy has got wind

27

of what we're trying to do. Then he lays it on the line for us. He tells us if you want to do anything like what we want to do, we got to go through the Big Boy. Otherwise nobody will touch us. We want to do business, we got to do it through the Big Boy.

"Well, you can figure we'd just about had it. As if we didn't have enough troubles, now we're going to have to cut this Big Boy in. So then Hal tells us we don't understand the situation. The Big Boy doesn't just sit back and collect his share. He earns it. Because he handles the job for us. He knows who to pay and what to pay for. We want the highway to go our way? He can fix it for us. When the highway commission gets all the reports in, they'll have no alternative but to lay that highway right where we want it. All we have to do is put the whole matter in his hands, sit back and relax.

"So I guess I can tell you, that made us feel a lot better. Things are looking up again. That's what we thought till he told us what is was going to cost. Sixty thousand dollars! That was the fee. Sixty grand and we get the highway. If we don't want to pay it, that's O.K. Then we have to take our chances. Except, of course, we can guess the chances aren't very good.

"So Hal leaves and we kick it around. We had a hot and heavy session that night, I can tell you. But in the end there wasn't any choice. What else are we going to do? What else would you do? Break the sixty grand down to cost per acre and my share is nine thousand dollars. That's no small potatoes, I can tell you, but figure that I've already been paid twenty-eight hundred in option money and I'm only sixty-two hundred out of pocket. And look what I stand to gain. Twenty-eight acres at two thousand each is fifty-six thousand dollars. That's forty-two thousand more than I paid for it, or a three hundred percent profit in less than two years. Knock off the nine grand I have to put up to insure the investment and I still make thirty-three thousand profit."

Fogarty got up and took a walk around the room. "Of course the big question is: How do I know I'll get anything for my sixty-two hundred dollars?

"I don't. Hal says the Big Boy always comes through, that that's the reason why he's the Big Boy—because he doesn't cheat. Well, we have to take his word for that. That's the chance I have to take. So what it boils down to is, I risk sixty-two hundred to make thirty-three thousand. To me that's worth a gamble any time.

"Sure there were a lot of squawks, but when I got out a pencil and paper and showed them, they all had to admit it made sense. And suppose the Big Boy doesn't come through,

Suppose he cheats us and I'm out my sixty-two hundred. I still have the land. Now it's cost me seven hundred and twenty-five an acre instead of five hundred but real estate's going up, The chances are I could sell it tomorrow for seven fifty. Anyway, a year from tomorrow.

"So Hal came down to see us again and we told him we'd go along with it and he told us to get the money together in cash and have it ready so that when the Big Boy wanted it, we could get it right to him. No delays. And he told us the way it was going to be was one man to make the delivery. He was to go up to Hartford all by himself with the money. So, of course, since George Demarest was the guy who had the connections and had brought all of this about, he was the obvious choice to do the delivering.

"So we start getting our cash together. Nothing bigger than a twenty, Hal told us, and it's all to go into a satchel. We take dough out of the bank in small amounts so nobody will notice. That's what Hal told us to do. He said that way nobody gets suspicious.

"So we're sitting on our dough and waiting and meeting every week and we're all pretty damned nervous. So finally the call comes in and we have a meeting at the Demarests'. That's the night we all bring our cash over and count it up and stick it in the satchel. That's the night I was telling you about this morning. August twenty-fourth. Wednesday night. The only thing wrong about what I told you this morning was that I gave him a check for an insurance policy. But I was protecting the other guys.

"Anyway, we get the money set and George is supposed to drive it to Hartford the next morning. We have a drink on that and we all go home and then we sit and wait.

"Well, we're all supposed to have dinner at George's the next night and hear the details. So we get there and the place is locked up tight and the car's gone. We figure George hasn't got home from Hartford yet but, like Carl says, 'Where's Deirdre?' She ought to've been home even if George wasn't. So we figure maybe she went with him. Hal said he was to come alone but maybe he eased up a little. So we go to Stan's house instead and we wait around and keep calling George's and getting no answer. The next day goes by and the next and gradually it dawns on us that this Demarest was a skunk. He got his hands on that sixty thousand dollars and he and Deirdre didn't make any trip to Hartford at all. They went the other way!

"So we talked about it and wondered what we could do. The others all said we couldn't do anything. All we can do is sit tight and hope maybe the highway will end up coming our way, that maybe the money got to the Big Boy after all. So that's what we did, sit tight. Then I got word from a guy in another construction company yesterday morning that the highway department has decided the road's going to go the *other* route. Keeping quiet isn't going to do any good any more." He turned to Fellows. "So you think Demarest wouldn't skip out, huh? You think he's off on a vacation? Well, now I guess you know better. Maybe he wouldn't scram with nine thousand dollars, but you up that to sixty and you got to admit that's a motive. Right?"

Fellows said, "Why didn't you come to the police earlier?"

"I just told you. We didn't want to rock the boat. How do we know Demarest didn't somehow get the money to the guy? We had to wait till we found out where the highway was going."

"Didn't it occur to you that a man carrying sixty thousand dollars in cash was running the risk of being robbed and maybe killed? Didn't it occur to you that Demarest might be in trouble?"

Yeah, but we didn't give it any real consideration. You remember I told you George canceled his milk deliveries? Carl Randolph had the bright idea of checking on that. And if you want to know something else, we, all of us, got into his house. It was locked up but he left a bedroom window open and we got the screen out and climbed in and we found out something else. They'd packed up and left."

"Oh, you did? I didn't find any open windows."

"We closed it."

Fellows looked at Wilks. "You got anything you want to ask, Sid?"

"One question. How much money did each person put into that satchel?"

Fogarty knew that answer backward. "Randolph's share was twenty thousand. Demarest's, fourteen thousand, fifty. Wilcox, eleven thousand five hundred and fifty. Mine was nine thousand, and Somers, fifty-four hundred."

"Everybody but Somers put in more than you?"

"Everybody but Stan had more acreage. We did it proportionally."

Wilks had his notebook out. "Randolph owned sixty-three acres, right? Demarest fourty-four, Wilcox thirty-six, you twenty-eight, and Somers seventeen. That right?"

"That's right."

Wilks wrote it down and said to Fellows, "That's all I wanted."

"All right, we'll go."

Fogarty got up. "Now wait, God damn it, you can't just walk on out. Say something. What're you going to do about it? That's what I want to know. That son of a bitch Demarest stole sixty thousand dollars!"

Fellows turned and regarded the burly man. "That's a pretty serious accusation you're making, Mr. Fogarty. I'd go easy if I were you."

"Easy? What are you trying to say, that he didn't steal it?"

"I don't know what he did. I don't know yet what any of you have done. We'll look into it," Fellows said, opened the door for Wilks and followed him out.

Fellows made a face. "It's easy to see why they've been keeping quiet. They'd rather take the loss than say what the money was for."

"All except Fogarty. I wonder what Demarest *did* do."

"So do I. Fogarty thinks because the sum is sixty thousand rather than nine it changes everything. If Demarest took it, he's still leaving more than that behind—his job, his reputation, his office equipment, a twenty-five thousand dollar house, forty-four acres of real estate worth, perhaps, another twenty-five, one car, a house full of furniture, and I don't know what else. Before we start issuing any alarms for him I'm going to want to hear what the others in that group have to say—especially that Carl Randolph."

"They probably won't want to say much, but I'll get it out of them. First thing in the morning."

6

At nine o'clock Friday morning, Detective Lieutenant Sidney Wilks rang the bell of the stately Carleton Randolph mansion on Cobblers Lane. It was Mrs. Randolph who answered. "Lieutenant Wilks," she said with a soft, Charleston accent. "It was so nice to get your call. Carl and I are just having coffee. Do come and have some with us."

She brought the detective into a spotless kitchen where, in a large breakfast area, Carleton Randolph sat over his coffee. "This is Lieutenant Wilks, Carl," she said. "Sit right here, Lieutenant, and I'll pour some coffee."

Randolph rose slowly and put his napkin aside to shake

hands. He was almost as tall as Wilks, gray and balding, a man in his late forties grown big around the waist.

"Here you are, Lieutenant," Mrs. Randolph said, setting a fresh cup and saucer before him and pouring from an electric pot on the table.

Randolph stared into his coffee and drained it quickly. "Lieutenant," he said, "your phone call puzzled us. This is the first time a policeman's ever set foot in this house. I can't imagine what's on your mind—what on earth you'd want with us?"

Wilks didn't choose to waste time fencing. "We're investigating the claim that George Demarest stole sixty thousand dollars from you and three other men. I want to see if you will verify this and, if you will, what you can tell us that will help us find him."

Randolph had suspected the visit had to do with Demarest, but he wasn't prepared to have it put to him all at once. He looked at Dixie and she looked at him and for a long moment he didn't move at all.

Finally he coughed. Then he breathed. Then he said, "Well, heh, that's quite a statement."

"It's a very serious charge. I want to know how much truth there is in it."

"Who made it, may I ask?"

"That's not to the question, Mr. Randolph. The question is, Did George Demarest disappear with sixty thousand dollars, twenty thousand of which belonged to you?"

"Twenty thousand, eh?"

"That's the figure we've been given."

"And there were three other men?"

"Warren, Wilcox, Stanley Somers who, we understand, is a cousin of yours, and Daniel Fogarty, a contractor in town. I'll ask you again. Is this true?"

Randolph wasn't happy about the question. "Well, you seem to know that already."

"And you gave George Demarest twenty thousand dollars in cash on the evening of August twenty-fourth, which he was supposed to take to Hartford the next day?"

Randolph said hastily, "Yes, and I want to explain about that. You see, the five of us got together. We sort of formed a committee—a civic committee. We believed it was important for the future development of Stockford that we have easier access to important points—the big cities around, the Merritt Parkway and the turnpike. The town has a Planning and Zoning Commission, of course, but they don't see the big picture. They don't think in terms like that. That's why we formed this committee. We wanted to agitate for a highway near Stockford. Of course, to do that, you have to lobby. And lobbying costs money. Quite a lot of money. This is what we collected the money for. The future of Stockford means a lot to the people who live here and we wanted to see our town grow, even if it meant using our own money to help get the job done."

Wilks listened with a stony face and then said, "That's not the way we heard it. We understand that Persall Brothers would pay two thousand an acre for land you all owned if the highway went by it."

Randolph moistened his lips, started to speak and said nothing.

Wilks went on. "And on the night of August twenty-fourth, you, Somers, Wilcox and Fogarty met at Demarest's house and gave him nearly forty-six thousand dollars in cash and he added another fourteen thousand himself, which money Demarest was to deliver to someone called Hal or to someone called the Big Boy the next day in order to get the highway to go by your land, is that right?"

This time Randolph did speak. "I don't think you've got it quite right, Lieutenant. This money was to set up a lobby in Hartford. A highway is needed in this area and we were pushing for it. That's perfectly legal. You have a program you want to see passed, you lobby for it. It's done all the time. You try to use all the influence you can muster to get the government to see the light. That's what the money was for. Those people you mentioned are people who know the ins and outs of lobbying. They were going to set it up for us."

"Call it lobbying, call it whatever you want, that was the arrangement, isn't that so? Demarest was going to deliver the money the next day to either Hal or the Big Boy to try to get the highway to go a certain way?"

Randolph admitted it. "Yes, They arrange lobbies. It's their business."

Wilks let that one pass. "Who was Demarest supposed to give the money to, the man called Hal, or the Big Boy?"

Randolph worked his lips. "I'm not sure. I don't know." He was flushed and uncomfortable. "Hal was going to call George in the morning and make arrangements. That was my understanding."

"And you don't know Hal's last name or who the Big Boy is?"

Randolph got a little redder. "No. George knew them, though. He know who they were. He was the one handling the arrangements. For the lobby."

Wilks turned to Mrs. Randolph. She was white, but she wasn't squirming like her husband. "Anything you can add to this? Anything you know about those people?"

She managed a saucy smile. "Oh, now, Lieutenant, you do flatter me. But I'm afraid I just don't bother my little head with business matters. Figures just fluster me to pieces so I'm afraid you'll have to ask Carl about anything having to do with money. He's the business head in the family."

Wilks got out his notebook and flipped it open to make quick jottings on a new page. "Now then, it appears that the Demarests, both husband and wife, went away the next day, taking the sixty thousand dollars with them. At least neither they nor the money have been seen since. Is that right?"

Randolph breathed a little easier. The lieutenant had finally got off that other subject. "I'm afraid so."

"And the money was not delivered to Hal or the Big Boy?"

"So far as we know."

"At least the highway isn't going to go by your land and Persall Brothers won't be exercising their option, right?"

"I don't know where the highway's going. I haven't heard about that. And I certainly don't know about the option you mention."

"You mean the highway still might go by Stockford?"

"I think there's still a good chance."

"I see." Wilks made cryptic notes indicating that Fogarty apparently hadn't told Randolph yet that they'd lost out. "Now the question is," he said, looking up again, "Did the Demarests steal this money? What's your view on that, Mr. Randolph?"

"I don't know what else you'd call it."

"Did they look like thieves to either one of you?"

Dixie waited for her husband to answer. He said, "Offhand they didn't look like thieves. We wouldn't have had anything to do with them if they had. No, they didn't look like thieves."

Wilks turned and Dixie said, "They surely seemed like very respectable people, Lieutenant. But then, I'm afraid I'm a terrible judge of character. If a man dresses well and is nicely mannered, why I just automatically assume he's a gentleman."

"And no one in the group, at any time, had any misgivings about trusting that much cash to Demarest?"

Both of the Randolphs shook their heads.

"But, despite this, you still think he stole the money?"

Randolph said bitterly, "Well, what the hell else could he have done with it? And don't try to make me believe Hal or the Big Boy grabbed the dough and scared them out of town because my imagination doesn't stretch that far. He was supposed to take that money to Hartford alone, not with his wife and his luggage. It's obvious they never went near Hartford. They lit out in some other direction—probably as soon as we left their house. They probably had the car already packed."

"And twenty thousand dollars of the money they took was yours?"

"Yes."

"Why didn't you report that to the police?"

Randolph started slightly and recovered with a shrug. "What good would that do?"

"It might get your money back."

"How would it? The money was in cash. Even if you caught him, how could I prove he took it?"

"Isn't the real reason you didn't report it that you didn't want to say what the money was for?"

"No, sir," Randolph said, coming back strongly. "I've got nothing to hide about that. The money was to lobby for a highway. There's nothing wrong in lobbying for legislation. Stockford needs a highway!"

"And you were hoping to sell your land."

"All right, so what if I was? There's nothing wrong in trying to make a buck, is there? So we lobby to get the highway to go our way. What do you think people lobby for anyway? To get something they *don't* want?"

"And then Demarest steals twenty thousand dollars from you and you don't do a thing about it?"

"I just told you. He takes off and who's going to catch him? It's goodbye money. There's practically no chance of getting any of it back and I'm not one to waste time and effort on futile programs. There's nothing to do but take your licking and learn a lesson."

Wilks said, "You're all smart businessmen—you and Fogarty especially. Why did it never occur to you he might take the money and run?"

Randolph frowned. "Why? Well, why should he? All right, let's admit we stood to make a pile if the highway went our way. He was as interested in that as any of us. Hell, his own profit on the deal would be *more* than sixty thousand. Who'd expect him to give all that up?"

"But even so you're convinced that's just what he's done?"

"What else? He's gone, isn't he?"

"He's gone, but he's left a house behind, his job, his forty-four acres, and the profit. As you just pointed out, he's left more than he's taken. Why would he do that?"

"He didn't leave his wife behind."

Wilks looked up from his notes. "What's that mean?"

"It means that maybe he wanted to get her out of here and sixty thousand dollars in cash would let him."

"Why would he want that?"

Randolph reached to pour himself more coffee. "Hell, I don't know."

"You said it. What are you holding back?"

Randolph set the pot down carefully and busied himself with cream and sugar. "It's my guess his wife was carrying on."

"With others in the group?"

"I wouldn't know about that."

"With Stan Somers and Warren Wilcox?"

"I wouldn't really know."

"You must have some reason for believing she was carrying on."

"No real reason. She just looked like the type, that's all."

Wilks turned. "What about you, Mrs. Randolph? Do you think Deirdre was carrying on with Somers and Wilcox?"

She smiled. "Really, Lieutenant, I plain don't know about things like that. I'm afraid I just never notice the ugly side of life. I suppose there are men and women who do things like that but I wouldn't ever suspect my friends of it."

"Then what reason would you give for Demarest running off with all that money?"

"I think it was temptation. All that money right there in your hands?" She gestured disarmingly. "You know, Lieutenant, like bank clerks embezzling. It's foolish and you always lose more than you gain, but some people just don't stop to think in moments like that. I suspect, Lieutenant, that right now George is very sorry for what he did. I suspect he'd give anything if he could bring the money back."

Wilks said, "And it's our job to see that he does bring it back. And it's your job to tell us everything you can that will help." He questioned them then on what they knew about George and his wife, their interests and hobbies, relatives and friends, the car they drove, their personal appearance.

Relatives and friends were subjects that hadn't come up in their association and the Randolphs couldn't help there. They didn't know where either George or Deirdre had originally come from. The couple had been married two years, they drove a tan 1966 Thunderbird, purchased the previous December. The Randolphs didn't know the license number.

"Demarest was doing pretty well in the insurance business then?"

"He seemed to be. Of course that's something you can never tell about these days, but I'd have to guess he was in the chips."

Randolph described the man as good-looking, good physical condition, a shade under six feet, sandy hair, blue or brown eyes—he wasn't sure. "Good personality, good mixer. You know, a good salesman type."

"Attractive to women?"

"I'd guess so but that's Dixie's department. How about it, Honey, would you call him attractive?"

Dixie nodded. "In a wholesome kind of way. Little boy kind of way. Not the suave kind of attraction—like Warren, for example."

"Marks or scars?" Wilks asked.

Neither knew of any. "He did wear a wedding ring," Randolph told him. "And a pretty handsome wristwatch. Can't tell you what it was like exactly, except it looked like gold. I'd guess it cost a good hundred and fifty dollars."

Deirdre Demarest was described as slight, five-three, dark, quite striking looking, possessed of a sultry, sulky air. "She'd never say much," Randolph noted. "Hardly ever smiled. You knew she was around, though. She had a certain appeal. She had a way of looking at a man."

Dixie said, "I'm surely glad to hear she looked at somebody. She certainly didn't look at the women."

Wilks said, "Did Demarest know about her affairs?"

Randolph guessed he did. "I told you I thought that was why he took the money. To get her away."

"You think he'd rather take her away than throw her out?"

"I think he was really stuck on the girl. I don't mean he showed it, I mean he didn't get mad at the way she behaved toward other men."

"What about him? Was he carrying on?"

Both Randolph and Dixie disclaimed any knowledge of such a thing.

"What about him and Mary Fogarty?"

"That was nothing. Mary played up to him some but that's as far as it went. So far as I know." Randolph frowned a little. "Of course we're not really in a position to say anything on that score. You have to realize, we never knew the Demarests before last fall and our relationship, while friendly, was essentially a business one."

7

Dr. Warren Wilcox, psychiatrist, was next on Wilks' check-out list. He had his office on the second floor of the Douden Building on Center Street, around the corner from police headquarters. He would be free, he had said in response to Wilks' phone call, between eleven and twelve.

The Douden Building was a small brick and stone structure, four floors high with two offices on a floor. A dentist had the rear office on the second floor and the psychiatrist the one in front. There was a small reception room off the elevator and a large, well-appointed suite off that, overlooking the busy street. An attractive girl of about twenty-three occupied the reception desk and oozed empathy.

She rose and opened the nearby door, and Wilcox came forward holding out a hand. "I believe your call has to do with your profession and not mine? Tell me what I've done and I'll make restitution. Did I pass a red light or park in a no parking zone?"

"I wouldn't know. Traffic violations isn't my department. What I'm here for is to ask your help in the matter of George Demarest's disappearance. I understand you're a friend of his."

"Of George?" Wilcox's eyes widened slightly. "He's supposed to have disappeared?"

"You didn't know?"

"I knew he and Deirdre went away. I supposed it was vacation. I wasn't thinking about it as a disappearance."

"And you didn't know he took sixty thousand dollars with him? And that eleven thousand five hundred and fifty dollars of it was supposed to belong to you?"

"What's this?" Wilcox asked. "What are you trying to say?"

Wilks sighed. "We can save the fencing if I tell you the police know about the action you and Carleton Randolph, Stanley Somers, Dan Fogarty and Demarest were taking with regard to the highway. Demarest was supposed to take sixty thousand dollars in cash up to Hartford on August twenty-fifth. Neither he nor his wife have been seen since and the testimony we've heard so far indicates that none of you believe he went off on any vacation. You think he stole that money and fled. Isn't that so, Doctor?"

Wilcox smiled. "Well, I can see you're too smart for me,

Yes, the fact of the matter is, George and Deirdre have run away with our money. How did you happen to find this out?"

"That's neither here nor there. The point is, do you want to help find him and get your money back?"

"Somebody complained, didn't they? I can guess who it was. That cluck, Fogarty."

"Cluck? You think a man is a cluck because he wants his money back?"

Wilcox smiled. "So it *was* Fogarty. I thought so. No, Lieutenant, I don't think a man's a cluck for wanting his money back. I only said that to test your reaction. I wanted to find out who it was and you didn't want to tell me. I laid a little trap for you, that's all." He laughed and clapped Wilks on the shoulder. "Don't be chagrined, Lieutenant. People's minds is my business. How they'll react and what will spur them to reaction is my field. In fact, I've written a book on it."

Wilks said, "That's good. Maybe it can answer my next question which is: If a man isn't a cluck for wanting his money back, why haven't you been complaining to the police too?"

"The answer to that is simple too. I'm a busy man. I've got more patients than I can handle. And, incidentally, I make more money than I can spend. To me, all the red tape involved in trying to interest the police in finding George Demarest—in the faint hope that I might be able to recover a small portion of my eight thousand dollars—isn't worth my time and energy."

"Eight thousand? I understood it was eleven and a half thousand."

"Seventy-nine hundred and fifty dollars is what it is. I'm deducting the thirty-six hundred Persall Brothers paid me in option money."

"Then if we find Demarest, you'll refuse to prosecute?"

Wilcox sat down in the easy chair under the lamp again. "I don't see any point, Lieutenant. Suppose you finally find him, say six months, a year, two years from now. How much of that money do you think he'll have left? And since it was all cash, I don't frankly see how we could prove he stole it. About all I can see coming out of this whole thing would be putting George in jail and I certainly don't see how that's going to do me any good. In fact, as a psychiatrist, I might find myself in the position of believing he's innocent—not legally, perhaps, but a victim of his own psychoses and neuroses. He probably needs help, not a jail sentence."

"You're taking your loss pretty well, I must say."

"As I mentioned before, it's only money. The only people

who'll suffer from the loss are my children. It'll cut their inheritance a little. But since there are three children to divide it between and since inheritance taxes are heavy, the difference will be scarcely noticeable."

Wilks said, "Well, there are people involved who would like to prosecute and it's the police department's job to try to find George Demarest. Therefore I'd like to know what you can tell me about him."

"Only him? Not her?" He waved at the facing leather couch. "Do sit down. It won't bite you. I won't make you lie on it. I'm well aware this is a case of *my* doing the talking, not the visitor."

Wilks sat a little gingerly and poised his pencil, "Both him and her, Doctor. Everything you can tell me."

"All right. Physically, George is youthful in appearance. I don't really know his age. Middle thirties, I'd guess. Sandy hair and coloring, a little shorter than I, a bit heavier. As for the wife, she's very young. Very early twenties. I believe she was a waitress when George met her, He was married to Jerry Somers at the time."

"I understand she has her eye on the men."

"This I wouldn't know anything about. She hasn't much in the brains department."

"I thought you had her pretty well figured. Your experience and all—"

Wilcox smiled. "Well, of course, speaking in generalities, I would expect a certain tramp quality in women of her type. If I'd psychoanalyzed her I'd be in a better position to render judgments."

"I was hoping you could be more specific. We've been told somewhere along the line that she rather had her eye on you."

"On me?"

"You find that extraordinary? I imagine a lot of women have an eye on you."

Wilcox liked that. He chuckled. "I see what you mean. Yes, I expect I attracted her somewhat. But you referred to her having an eye on 'men.' I took you to mean generically, that she was interested in the male of the species."

"Was she?"

"I think it quite likely. But I can't say for sure."

"What about her interest in you?"

"A passing fancy. If you could even call it that."

"How far did this passing fancy go?"

Wilcox spread his long fingers. "Let us say there was a feeling in the air. I could sense an interest. I might add I could sense that it was an interest I could have pursued had I been so inclined. But I'm a married man with a family. I also have a reputation in this community. That sort of thing is not for me."

"Do you think something like that would have been for any of the other men you know about?"

"I wouldn't really have any idea."

Wilks thumbed back a page in the notebook and frowned. "You said something interesting a minute ago. You said Deirdre was Demarest's second wife—"

"Yes."

"And that he was married to a Jerry Somers at the time. Do you mean Stanley Somers' wife?"

"She's now Somers' wife. She had been George's. I don't know when or anything like that."

"So Demarest was married to Jerry, he meets Deirdre, divorces Jerry, marries Deirdre. Jerry marries Stan Somers, and then the four of them get thrown together by this deal you were all in?"

"That appears to be what happened."

"How was it working out?"

"You mean, did Jerry have the knives out for Deirdre? Not that I noticed. I'll admit she and George seemed pretty cool toward each other."

"But she didn't make life a hell for Deirdre?"

"No. Why?"

"We're looking for the reason Demarest took advantage of the accident that put sixty thousand dollars into his hands and caused him and Deirdre to pack up and flee, leaving everything else behind. It would have to be a pretty strong motive." Wilks looked at the psychiatrist. "You any suggestions."

"Yes. The obvious one."

"Which is?"

"Sixty thousand dollars, of course."

"You think he needed that money? The others we've talked to seem to think Demarest was pretty well fixed."

Wilcox said, "It's only a guess, but if you want my guess, I don't think he was. He sells insurance and I expect he does pretty well at it. But if you knew George and you're in my field, you can size him up and say, this is a man with an inferiority complex. He's compensating. And the way he's compensating is by extending himself, always trying to associate with those who are higher up the economic ladder than he is, trying to match those people, match their standard of living, persuade the world that he's better than he is. Look at the house he's got. It's a twenty-five thousand dollar house.

41

Two cars, a new Thunderbird last year. He belongs to the right clubs. He serves the best booze—and lets you know it's the best. He lives just about as well as I do and you know he can't begin to match my income. It's my guess George was in over his head and saw that sixty thousand dollars as the way out."

Wilks said, "Well, that could be, except for one thing. He owned forty-four acres of that property Persall Brothers wanted—"

"He did? You mean clear of mortgages?"

"I don't know about that. You're probably right. More likely the bank owned it and he was paying off on a mortgage. But what I mean is, if Persall Brothers bought it, he'd make sixty thousand dollars in profit."

"That's 'if' Persall Brothers bought it."

"My understanding is that if Demarest delivered that sixty thousand dollars to someone in Hartford called the Big Boy, the highway would have gone where you wanted and Persall Brothers would have bought it."

"That's what we all thought and that's why we all went along with it. But George and Deirdre disappearing with the money puts a different slant on the whole thing."

"How's that?"

Wilcox leaned forward. "All right, you seem to know the whole story so there's no point kidding around. Once we found the highway might go another route we got pretty discouraged. We were pretty sure it would. So who was it persuaded us that for sixty thousand dollars it would go our way? Some nondescript man who called himself Hal and who claimed he was a go-between for somebody even more obscure —someone calling himself the Big Boy. And who was it who brought Hal down from Hartford? Who was it who handled all the negotiations? It was George. And who was the obvious choice to handle the money? George. So, Lieutenant, why should we believe there's any Big Boy at all? Why should we believe that this unidentifiable Hal is any more than somebody George hired to trick us into parting with our money?"

"So you think that's what happened?"

"I think that's exactly what happened. I think George was strapped, that he was banking everything on selling the land. And when he saw the sale probably wasn't going through, he dreamed up this plan. I don't think he just suddenly saw all this money and couldn't resist the temptation to run off with it. I think he had this worked out all along."

Wilks compressed his lips and pondered while he wrote. "That's an interesting angle," he said. "That's one the Ran-

42

dolphs didn't come up with."

"Carl wouldn't. I don't mean he isn't bright enough, but he'd have a mental block. His brain wouldn't let him conceive of such an idea."

"Oh? How so?"

"Carl fancies himself a very shrewd real estate man. If my theory is correct, he was cheated out of twenty thousand dollars on a real estate deal. In his own field. Psychologically he wouldn't be able to live with such an idea. Therefore his brain wouldn't present it to him and I daresay that if it were presented by someone else, he would reject it angrily."

"But being cheated doesn't bother you?"

"Let's say I'm not unnecessarily bothered. I was cheated in a field about which I know nothing. I'd be an easy mark so this doesn't damage my ego unduly. If it were in my own field, then I expect I'd react the same way Carl would. Our egos need to be upheld, Lieutenant."

"I suppose so." Wilks got back to his own field. "One thing. There was a meeting at George Demarest's house on August twenty-fourth when you all put up the money. His share was supposed to be fourteen thousand and fifty dollars. Did he actually have that money himself or did he say he'd throw his share in when he delivered the money?"

"He had it in cash himself." Wilcox sat back. "I would suspect that George, having this plan in mind, converted every asset he could possibly lay his hand on into cash. He was probably clever enough to find out how much cash he could raise before he set a price on the rest of us. If he could have only raised seven thousand, for example, he probably would have told Hal to make the price thirty thousand. If he could have raised more than fourteen for his share, I expect he would have raised our shares accordingly.

"But of course, I'm only theorizing. I'm only guessing he was pressed for funds judging from what he did and the kind of man he struck me to be. Maybe I'm all wrong. Maybe George had an inheritance somewhere and he's rolling in money and there really is a Big Boy and Demarest's efforts were to show us all what a big operator he is. And maybe the Big Boy killed him so he couldn't talk. But then, that's a field you'd know better than I."

Wilks said, "I understand that before this Hal came on the scene you people talked with some other people Demarest brought around, people connected with soil testing or surveying or engineering firms."

"Yes. Or at least that's what they were supposed to be. George brought them in too. The idea was to see what the

43

chances were of the highway going our way."

"Did these people have last names? Were they identified at all?"

"Yes, they had last names." Wilcox sat up. "I don't know if they were the people they said they were, though. After George disappeared with the money Carl Randolph tried to get hold of one or two of those people. He found people with those names connected with those firms all right but those people didn't know him. They claimed they didn't know what he was talking about. It's my theory the ones we met were impostors—some more stooges George brought in. What is it you call this sort of thing, Lieutenant? A con game? I guess this is about the biggest con game you've ever seen, isn't it?"

"Around here," Wilks admitted. "If that's what it really is."

8

The chief was out, Chernoff told Wilks when he returned to headquarters. He'd gone to the bank to see the credit manager at half-past nine and wasn't back yet. "Kettleman got the dope on Demarest's car," Chernoff went on. "We can put it on the wires any time you want."

"Any time the chief wants. He get in touch with the insurance company in Hartford?"

"He called them. I don't know what he got. Did Demarest really run off with the money?"

"Fogarty's story stands up. Sixty thousand dollars and George Demarest seem to be missing. So far that's all I know."

"You think they could all be lying?"

Wilks looked at him. "Where'd you get that idea?"

"Well, Fogarty lied yesterday, didn't he? And if the way I understand it is right, that they gave Demarest cash and they can't prove they gave it to him, we can't prove they did either. They can say anything they want."

Fellows opened the door then and came in. Wilks repeated Chernoff's idea to him. "I admit," Wilks added, "that theory is as good as some of the others I've heard."

Fellows opened the door to his office. "Well, come on in and tell me what you did hear. You talk to them all?"

"Only to Randolph and Wilcox. I called up Somers, of

course, but his wife said he's in New York Thursdays, Fridays and Saturdays working on rehearsals and taping of the show he writes for. I'm going to want to talk to her though, this afternoon. I learned she used to be married to George Demarest."

"So I found out too." Fellows sat down at his desk and swung his chair around. "What'd Randolph and Wilcox have to say?"

"They tried to whitewash the bribe attempt but confessed to being fleeced. Fogarty seems to be telling the truth about that at least. You want it blow-by-blow?"

Fellows nodded. "I want the whole thing. I want everything they told you about Demarest and his wife and the relationship of the group and all the nuances."

Wilks got out his notebook and started a recapitulation and the chief listened in silence. Wilks finished and closed his notebook. "So you get three theories. One from Randolph that Demarest was jealous of his wife and used the sixty thousand to get her away from a den of wolves—presumably to put her in another den somewhere else. There's Mrs. Randolph's theory that he couldn't resist the temptation of all that cash. And there's Wilcox's idea that Demarest was on the edge of bankruptcy and plotted the whole thing to get the means to desert his creditors. Then there's Chernoff's theory that Demarest merely went away on vacation and his friends cooked up the whole thing to blacken his reputation. And I suppose Mrs. Somers will say the Demarests fled to get away from her—after the land deal threw them together again."

"And you don't like any of them?"

Wilks shook his head. "There're too many holes, Fred. Take Randolph's theory. Let's say Demarest is so crazy about Deirdre that he divorces his wife to marry her. Let's say she can't stay away from the men. Maybe he would try to take her away from temptation rather than throw her out. And maybe, if he was desperate, that sixty thousand would look pretty good to him. Even so, no matter how you paint it, it's hard to imagine the guy going off the deep end so far as to grab sixty thousand in cash and leave more than that behind. Seems to me, if he wanted to get his wife out of range, he'd sell out and make a normal move. At least if he's a normal man, and I have to figure insurance salesmen as being about as normal as you're going to find.

"Then there's the Wilcox theory. He's going bankrupt and sees a way to con his friends out of forty-six thousand dollars. He converts everything he's got into another fourteen, hires guys to put on an act about the Big Boy, gets the money and

45

takes off. That's pretty elaborate scheming for an amateur. It would take more brass and aplomb than I'd expect a man to have on his first try."

Wilks said, "Forget the temptation idea—that when he saw all that cash he grabbed it and ran. That's like saying a man is tempted to jump out the window. Those other two are the only theories that sound even plausible to me and I don't like either one."

Fellows said, "You think of any you like better?"

"I'd like robbery better, except you're not going to pack up your suitcases, lock up the house and drive off to get robbed. No. They meant to take off with the money and, judging from the icebox full of food they left behind, it was a sudden decision." He shook his head and then eyed the chief. "You don't look overly disturbed about it. What have you been finding out?"

Fellows said, "I think I've been finding out what really went on."

"Oh? So? Where?"

"First, I called up the insurance company in Hartford that Demarest represents. Talked to some vice-president—fellow named Armbruster—and he was pretty alarmed. In fact, he's coming down this afternoon. He's afraid Demarest might not only have gone off with the sixty thousand we're talking about, he might have taken about a month's worth of premium checks. They haven't heard from Demarest in over three weeks and haven't been able to reach him and they've been getting worried."

"Then he hadn't talked vacation to them or anything?"

"No."

"How much does he think Demarest might have made off with?"

"He didn't quote any figure, but he told me Demarest has been averaging twelve to fifteen thousand a year in the insurance business—that's net, not gross. So gross income might be fifteen hundred a month, roughly. That's his commission so you can guess the actual money he takes in would run five to ten times that much. Anyway, it's enough to have Armbruster and company pretty worried. They want to get hold of Demarest's books.

"It took a while but I finally got him quieted down enough to give me some details about Demarest. He had a very good year in 1962—back when he bought that property. He made twenty-one thousand. Then he made fifteen thousand in '63, nine thousand in '64, eleven thousand in '65 and he'd earned ten thousand five hundred thus far this year."

"His earnings sure fluctuate."

"Since 1962 they have. Before that, they were coming up in a steady curve. Sixty-two was the high point and the company has been a little disappointed in the fall-off since then."

Wilks stroked his chin. "Even what he's been making since isn't bad for a guy with no children. I wish Marge and I made that kind of dough."

"I wish I made it *with* children. Anyway, I found out from Armbruster where Demarest is from, family and things. They're up outside of Boston and we'll see if the police there can get anything on him. It looks as if the Demarests went south, judging from the winter clothes they left behind, but the family might have information on what places they like down there."

"Well that helps."

"And they've got pictures of Demarest in their files and his own insurance policy. That's for fifty thousand and that's where I found out he'd changed wives two years ago.

"So then I went over to the Stockford National Bank and talked to Ben Grayson and Ben gave me a picture of Demarest's financial condition. At least what he knows about it." Fellows compressed his lips. "Wilcox had a good hunch. Demarest was in trouble."

"These psychiatrists are too damned smart. All the time I was talking to him I had the feeling he was mind-reading me."

"Well, I'd say Wilcox was only half-right on that living-beyond-his-means bit. Demarest may have been doing that recently, but he doesn't seem to have started out that way. Grayson knows Demarest somewhat and he gave me some background. Demarest married his first wife, the present Mrs. Somers, back in 1960. Her maiden name was Geraldine Barker. And he bought a house for them. It's the one the Somerses now live in. He made close to thirteen thousand that year and his five-year average with the insurance company was eleven-five and it was climbing yearly. He also had six thousand dollars in a savings account and about four thousand in stocks.

"The cost of the house was twenty-eight five, well within his means, and he made a big down payment and was paying off the balance at a faster rate than he had to.

"Then, in 1962, he bought the land with the bank's help. He put seven thousand down and again started paying off faster than he had to.

"In 1964 he took on a second house—the one he and Deirdre had. This one cost him twenty-four two, and this time he made a small down payment and took out a long-term mortgage. Twenty-five years."

"He was starting to hurt."

"It seems so. Even so, he bought the Thunderbird last year. The bank didn't handle that one. Then, this past year he began falling behind in his payments on what the bank's holding. He's three months behind right now—in everything—and the bank's been getting after him."

"Three months? Sounds like he was putting it into that fourteen thousand bribe."

"Probably. Because, before he got so far behind, he approached the bank for a loan. He told them it was for investment purposes but it was probably for the bribe because he promised to have it paid back in a year. But money's tighter now and he was already carrying a heavy financial burden, his income was fluctuating, he was falling behind in his payments, his savings account was closed out and, to top it off, he wasn't at all clear on what the investment was. The bank turned him down.

"He got the money somewhere else, obviously, but he didn't get it from them."

Wilks said, "That fluctuating income started with the divorce and the second wife. Sounds like he didn't get as much work done with Deirdre around. Maybe he had to watch her too much."

"It sounds as though things weren't as smooth as they were before," Fellows agreed. "Anyway, that and the second house gave me the idea. Grayson said Dave Stottlemeyer was the lawyer who handled the divorce. You know Dave. So I went over to talk to him. He didn't want to reveal much about his client's business despite Demarest's being missing with all that money. But he did say it was Demarest who wanted the divorce, though he let his wife get it. She went to Reno in the summer of '64. Dave wouldn't give me figures but he said she bled him white for it. He had to sign over the first house and everything in it. Then there was cash and a percentage of his income till she remarried. She married again in December the same year which got him off the hook, but she left him very little to operate with and he must have been up to his neck in debt. So it's no wonder he was eager to sell the land."

Wilks nodded. "I can get that picture but I still can't see him rigging up the con game Wilcox has him doing."

"Not the way we have him painted so far, but I can see it another way. We've got him with a mortgage on the land, mortgage on his new house, payment on whatever kind of loan he had to get to pay off the first house for his wife. Then

48

there's the furniture for the new house, there's the Thunderbird he bought to keep up appearances plus the standard of living he's trying to maintain and, on top of that, there's the fourteen thousand he had to raise somehow as a bribe attempt. He's probably in so deep the only thing that can save him is the land sale.

"So let's say his life—at least his financial life—depends on the highway going by his property and Persall Brothers exercising their option. This depends on whoever the Big Boy is and that's a gamble. But he has no choice. But let him be picked to make the delivery and let him get sixty thousand in his hands and now he's got a choice. He can play it straight and gamble that he can be bailed out, or he can grab the sixty and leave everything behind and start over. And that's what he did."

Wilks said, "Putting temptation in that light, I guess I'll have to buy it."

"So now we'll put out the alarm."

"Right. Kettleman's got the info on the car, license, serial number and all. And that insurance guy, Armbruster, will bring down pictures of Demarest? What about his wife?"

"I don't have much on her yet. I looked her up in the town clerk's files and found she and Demarest got married on September 12, 1964. Her maiden name was Fredericks and she was born in New London in 1943."

"I'll contact the New London police. And I'm going to talk to the ex-wife. If Demarest ditched her for Deirdre and now has stolen fifty-four hundred dollars from her new husband, she ought to go all out helping us locate him."

9

Geraldine Somers dialed a number and drummed impatiently on the telephone table. A soft, slightly overdone female voice came on at the other end and said, "Doctor Wilcox's office. Good afternoon."

"This is Jerry Somers," she said abruptly. "I want to talk to the doctor."

"I can't disturb the doctor, Mrs.—"

Jerry's voice came up. "Listen, you frustrated Dracula, don't you try to put me off. Tell Wilcox to get on that phone or he's going to be very sorry."

The receptionist put down the phone and said into the intercom, distinctly enough so that Jerry could hear, "Doctor, Mrs. Somers is on the phone insisting on talking to you. She sounds highly neurotic."

There was a response and, in a moment, Wilcox asked the receptionist to go see that the patient was comfortable. He picked up the phone and said evenly, "Yes, Mrs. Somers?"

Jerry's voice was heated. "Don't you 'Mrs. Somers' me, you arthritic Romeo. And don't try hiding behind your receptionist's skirts. I know you're avoiding me, but you're not getting off that easily."

"Jerry," Wilcox answered soothingly, "you're full of hostilities. Things haven't been going well for you and you're lashing out at everyone to get rid of your frustrations. My advice—"

"I'm not calling you for advice. I'm giving you some. Stan didn't walk out on me because he doesn't like the way I comb my hair. He walked out because of you and I'm going to ask you again. What do you plan to do about it?"

"Now you can't fault me there, Jerry. Stan only left you last week and we haven't seen each other since August nineteenth. You're only imagining a connection."

"You'd better start thinking what you're going to do about it. It's all your fault. You're the one who operated the seductive line. You're the one who didn't want to stop when Stan threatened."

Wilcox said sharply, "Now you're being childish. You played with fire and you should have known better."

"I played with fire?"

"I don't mean with me. I mean you were so bitter against George that you practically threw Stan at Deirdre just so you could see George cuckolded. Then, when Stan started liking the idea too much, you became bitter toward him and tried cuckolding him with me."

"That's your interpretation," she snapped. "What really happened was you got so sore at Stan cutting you out with Deirdre that you tried to get back at him through me."

"Sore? Angry? At Stan?" Wilcox laughed. "Deirdre didn't throw me over. I threw her over."

"Of course that's what you'd say."

"Come now. Do you really think Stanley is a better lover than I am? He only joined the parade of men that passes through Deirdre's life. Deirdre is a girl who loves men. She's not like you, Jerry. You hate men. I turned to you because she bored me. There's more to a girl like you, Jerry. Knowing you has meaning."

"Sure it has meaning. So the moment Stan leaves me, so do you. Now you can divorce that whining shrew Moira and have somebody to turn to, why don't you?"

"Jerry, I have three boys. I have a responsibility to them. Until they're grown, I can't think of myself."

"Oh, you'd like me to wait? When will the youngest start college? Seven years from now, isn't it?"

Wilcox said sadly, "I can't ask you to wait, darling."

"You're goddam right about that, and I have quite a few more things to say and you'd better listen because they concern you. How would you like it, for example, if word of all your amours was made public? You'd better start wondering what it will do for your future."

"My dear girl, where's your evidence? Where's your proof?"

"Those nights in your office—"

"You mean those nights when I was working on my book?"

"Your book? That's a laugh."

"My book. Don't you realize that's why I haven't seen you recently? It's not that I don't care for you, Jerry. But the book is finished. That's why I couldn't see you that next week when Stan went to New York. I'd taken the manuscript into the publishers and I didn't have any more excuses to give Moira to go to the office at night."

"You're a God-damned liar. You told me that weekend it was waiting around for the Demarests and wondering where they'd gone with your dough that kept you honest. But that excuse can't last so now you have a new one."

"I swear to you, Jerry. I finished the book Wednesday night after we gave George the money and I took it in Thursday. The book is finished."

"Meaning and so are we?"

"I didn't say that, Jerry. I'm only pointing out that I can't pretend to Moira that I'm writing case histories in my office at night any more."

"I'll bet the best ones are the ones you're in. You not only listen to sex and practise sex, you even write about it. If you've got anything about me in that stinking book, I'll take you for every cent you own. You think you're clever but your excuses don't fool me any more than they fool Moira. She knows about us. Everybody in that cozy group knows about us. It's no more a secret than you and Deirdre were a secret. Anyway, what I really called to tell you was that some detective from the police department wants to talk to me. What do you think of that?"

"I think he probably wants to ask about George. The police

know what he did and are looking for him. They talked to me about that this noon."

"You didn't hear me straight. He called up this morning wanting Stan and I told him Stan's in New York. What I didn't tell him was that Stan isn't living here any more. He's staying at Carl's. But now he's called back and wants to talk to me! Not Stan. Me! So you give me one decent reason why I shouldn't spill the works to him."

"My dear girl, if you want to confess to him, go right ahead."

Jerry said, "Damn you. All right, you've been warned, Warren. I can tell him just what that money was for. I can tell him the lot of you were in collusion to commit bribery."

Wilcox sighed. "It's already been explained to the detective. He understands."

"He'll understand a lot more when I'm through."

"And what do you want for silence?" Wilcox asked wearily.

"Oh, I don't know what I want," Jerry said, suddenly close to tears. "I don't want being left alone and deserted. I don't want you and Stan walking out on me both at once."

"You're upset and lonely and you think it's the end of the world. But it's not. Stan'll come back."

"Not Stan! And I don't want him back. He went too far overboard for that bitch."

"There'll be other men, Jerry. You're a very attractive woman, you know."

Jerry's voice got snappish again. "That's right. Butter me up. And maybe I'll take my lickings quietly. Well, you'll see how quiet I'm going to be."

"You'll only make trouble for yourself. You know, Jerry, it might be good for you to see me professionally. I think I can help you."

"You lousy, stinking—" Jerry Somers slammed down the phone.

10

When Wilks arrived at Jerry Somers' house she welcomed him with a bright smile and an almost effusive manner, making him comfortable in the living room and assuring him she was delighted if she could help the police. She sat down facing him and said, "It's about George Demarest, I believe you said? Yes. Stan and I know him."

Wilks said, "I understand Mr. Demarest bought this house and the furniture too. They were paid for by him?"

Jerry sat up a little and took a quick, rather than languid puff on her cigarette.

"I believe you divorced Mr. Demarest in August of 1964 and both of you thereafter remarried."

"Yes," she said flatly.

"You married Stanley Somers in December of that year. And Mr. Demarest married Deirdre Fredericks soon after the divorce became final?"

"Not soon after, the *day* after the divorce became final."

"And am I correct in saying that you didn't see George again until last November?"

"That's right. George wasn't much of a social lion and that girl he married wouldn't help matters."

"Oh?" Wilks made notes. "I thought Mr. Demarest was supposed to belong to quite a few clubs and was quite active socially."

"He was active where he thought it might help his insurance business. He was social for business reasons and the business was mostly men business. When he and I were married, what social life we had was my doing. After he married that other woman I expect his social life stopped."

"Do you know much about her?"

"I can tell you she was a pushover for men. Any man. Any time, any place. She quit high school because she was pregnant. She had an abortion. She got thrown out of the house when she was seventeen because of her carryings-on. After that she knocked around, supporting herself with odd jobs, waitress work and the like, and had affairs with any man who cared to. Then my husband met her and fell under her spell and he left me for her. She's a clever one, that one."

"Is what you're telling me about her information, or hear-say?"

"Information. My lawyer dug it up when George wanted the divorce."

"We've had other people say she was stupid and ignorant."

Jerry snorted. "That sounds like Warren Wilcox. She wasn't stupid. She just didn't talk much. And I'm sure Warren never bothered to notice what kind of brains she had anyway. He's not interested in a girl's brains."

"Is that remark based on firsthand knowledge? I don't mean to insult you. I was wondering if he'd made passes."

"He tried. He didn't succeed. But that wouldn't keep him from trying."

"I see. How about the other women in the group? Mrs. Randolph and Mrs. Fogarty?"

"You'll have to ask them," she said. "I certainly would be surprised if he hasn't."

"But you can't say that he did?"

"No, I can't," she said shortly.

"You've given us a picture of the girl. Fast and loose, I guess is the way you'd characterize her. What about Mr. Demarest? What kind of a man was he?"

"Fast and loose too."

"Meaning he made a play for anything in skirts?"

"Yes."

"Then Deirdre wasn't the first girl he got involved with during your marriage?"

"No," she lied.

"Do you know the names of any other women he was involved with?"

She shook her head.

"But you do know there were other women? Something gave you reason to believe this?"

"The usual things. The lipstick on the handkerchiefs and shirt collars, the long hairs on his jackets."

"You ever talk about this with him?"

"No. I preferred to play dumb."

"I see. And when he wanted a divorce so he could marry Deirdre, you fought to keep him?"

"Who says *he* wanted the divorce? I divorced him. I'd had enough of his playing around."

"Oh. But you had your lawyer dig up evidence against Deirdre that would keep him from wanting to marry her. Why did you do that?"

The damned detective was infuriatingly hard to lie to. "Look," she said, "are you here to investigate me or George? I resent all these personal questions. I'll tell you anything you want to know about George and about all the others engaged in trying to bribe the highway department—"

"Bribe the highway department? I understood the aim was to bribe people who would report to the highway department."

"Well, whatever it was, it was bribery. And they were all in on it—George, Stan, Carl Randolph and that Dan Fogarty."

"And you didn't approve of it?"

"Of course I didn't. Bribery is a crime, isn't it? I didn't want any part of the whole shoddy mess."

"How about the other wives?"

"Oh, they were perfectly willing to go along."

"And you've just mentioned that your own husband was also willing to go along."

"Yes, that's right."

"With the 'whole shoddy mess'?"

"Yes."

"You don't trouble to excuse your husband nor defend him, I notice. Did you voice your disapproval to him?"

"Sure."

"And he wouldn't listen so you're perfectly willing to lump him in with the others and accuse him along with them?"

"He's in it. He can't deny it."

"Is there trouble between you and your husband?"

"What are you talking about?"

"I'm interested in your attitude toward him. Was he, by any chance, one of those interested in Deirdre Demarest?"

Jerry stood up. "If you ask any more questions about me, you can get the hell out of my house!"

Wilks rose and tried to be soothing. "I don't mean to be personal," he said, "but we're trying to find out all we can about George and Deirdre. I can assure you, Mrs. Somers, it's information that wouldn't go beyond the police department."

"Well ask Stan about Deirdre then. How would I know what they do?"

"I suppose her lipstick on his handkerchiefs and shirt collars or her hairs on his coat."

"Well I don't know of any. Stan would be smarter about that kind of thing than George anyway. He's had three wives before me."

"All right, I guess that's something we could ask him. Do you expect him home this evening?"

"You can't tell about Stan from Thursday through Saturday. It depends on what kind of problems they have with the show, how much rewriting has to be done. Sometimes he comes home Thursday and Friday nights. Most of the time, though, he stays in the director's apartment and is gone from Thursday morning till Saturday evening. Are you going to arrest him for bribery?"

"Right now what the sixty thousand dollars was for doesn't concern us, Mrs. Somers. All that concerns us is that George Demarest stole it. Do you have any pictures of him by the way? Pictures would help us identify them."

Jerry said, "Mr. Detective, if you think I'd knowingly let a picture of George Demarest exist anywhere where I could get at it, you're a kook."

"What about marks and scars?"

"The only mark he has on him is his social security number tattooed on the inside of his left arm near the shoulder."

When Wilks turned to go, Jerry was quick to rise and her manner was more friendly as she saw him to the door.

11

Slowly the wheels of police investigation began to turn and on Friday afternoon insurance executive Robert Armbruster appeared with pictures of George Demarest and all the data in the company files. Armbruster was nervous, worried and eager to help. "Anything we can do, Chief. There's a month's worth of insurance payments he hasn't turned in. This is very bad for the company."

On Saturday the wheels moved a little faster. It was Detective Sergeant Edward N. Lewis' day off but he spent it fingerprinting the Demarest house in an effort to determine, from the assortment he got, which prints belonged to George Demarest, which to his wife, and which had been left by friends and acquaintances. Patrolman Manny was talking to members of the clubs Demarest belonged to and Wilks was continuing the task of questioning the husbands and wives who had been robbed.

Results were still scanty by Saturday noon but Fellows called a press conference nevertheless. Publicity was what he was after for, in affairs involving fugitives, an alerted citizenry was the best hope for leads.

The press conference was attended by nine newsmen, representing the wire services, the area TV stations and neighboring dailies. The reporters recorded the information dutifully but the hunt was not where their interest lay. Richard Harrington, reporter for the *Pittsfield Chronicle*, flipped another page of his notebook and said, "So much for that. Now let's have the story."

Fellows said, "But that *is* the story."

"You've given us pictures and descriptions but no story. Here's a guy who's stolen sixty thousand dollars, and that's all you tell us. Who'd he steal it from? How'd he get hold of it?"

Fellows shook his head. "That's the tough part. That's information I can't give you. But," the chief went on, "I will tell you this. The complaint was registered by Daniel Fogarty of the Fogarty Construction Company. Why don't you talk to him?"

It wasn't that the chief didn't want the story to come out. "In fact," he said to Wilks later that afternoon, "I hope it does come out. But I can't be the one to tell it. It's better if that bunch puts their own feet into it. And they probably will."

Wilks wasn't so sure. "They probably won't," he said. "They're clamming up. The word's obviously been passed to know nothing."

"Oh?"

"I mean it. I've just been talking to Moira Wilcox. Got her while dashing Warren was out on the golf course. She claimed Demarest seemed like a nice chap and if he made passes at the ladies, she didn't know anything about it. And Deirdre was a nice, quiet girl, and a good hostess. Moira's a skinny, tense, nervous type and she was lying through her teeth. They're a tight little band now and so busy whitewashing each other they're even whitewashing the Demarests."

Wilks might have been right about the whitewashing, but the band wasn't as tightly cemented as it appeared. "I was interviewed by that detective this afternoon," Moira Wilcox said to her husband that evening. She waited for a reaction but all she got was a grunt and she tried again. "Well, aren't you interested in what I told him? I should think that would interest you a great deal."

"What did you tell him?"

"You're so sure I didn't tell him anything, aren't you? You're always so sure of yourself."

"What is there to tell him?" he asked innocently.

"You always pretend you're so pure, don't you? You think I don't know any better? You always count on my good nature."

That got a reaction. "Your good nature," he sneered.

"You think I'm not good natured? What do I have to endure? Only the shame and embarrassment of watching my husband make passes at other women. Everybody knows what you do. I know all about it and I suffer."

"That's just like you," Wilcox said wearily. "A paranoic. You're so basically insecure you go around looking for trouble where there isn't any. If I say hello to a woman you think it's a pass. If I work late in the office on my book you think I've got a woman there. The trouble is you're one of those unfortunate people who compensates for an inferiority complex by trying to tear everybody else down. Why don't you build yourself up instead?"

"Build myself up with what?" Moira came back. "What have you left me to build with? You've taken away my self-respect. You've taken away my faith in my own husband. Don't you think I've got a right to kick and complain? I'm not in your thoughts even when you're home. Your mind isn't ever on me and the children. It's on women and sex and what woman's going to come next."

"All right, believe what you want, but do you know why you want to believe it? Because, deep down in your sub-conscious you know what the reason would be. Ask yourself why you think I philander. Ask yourself what kind of a relationship we have together and ask yourself why. You can't enjoy life and it bugs you that I can. So you're going to do everything you can to make me as miserable as you are."

"Don't you think, if I really wanted to make life miserable for you, I couldn't do it? This afternoon for instance?"

"And how, this afternoon?"

"I could have told that detective all about you and Deirdre Demarest."

"All *what* about me and Deirdre Demarest?"

"That you and she were having an affair. That George even gave you a black eye for it."

"Oh, come off it."

"I'm not really so dumb you know. I never did believe that story about you tripping on the stairs coming down from the office after an evening of working on your book. I happened to call the office that night and there was nobody there. So you were lying and I knew then that George gave it to you. Because that was when you were still seeing that woman—before you got so interested in Jerry Somers."

"Oh my God. Deirdre and Warren. Jerry and Warren. How about Dixie Randolph and Warren? And let's not forget Mary Fogarty and Warren."

"That's right. Laugh about your infidelities while you throw them in my face. You think that detective wouldn't be interested to know you were having an affair with George's wife? You don't think that might have something to do with George's going away?"

"He went away because he had sixty thousand dollars in his pockets."

"That's what you say. I say he wouldn't run off with that money and leave all the land behind. I say he had another reason and it wouldn't surprise me one bit if that reason was you and Deirdre."

"Me and Deirdre? I thought you had it argued that I'd stopped having an affair with her and was having an affair with Jerry Somers at the time George took the money."

"All right, maybe it was because first you had an affair with her and then Stan had an affair with her."

"Oh, so now Stan was having an affair with her too?"

"Are you pretending you didn't know Stan was carrying on with Deirdre?"

Wilcox shook his head. "God, you really ought to stop watching so much television. You're getting so you see sex everywhere."

12

Sunday morning brought the first break in the case when Staten Island police produced George Demarest's 1966 Thunderbird. They said it had been reported to them on September second as having been left standing for several days without license plates in front of the home of a Mrs. Nathan Agronski a few blocks from the ferry terminal.

They had therefore impounded the car, checked it against stolen car lists, opened the trunk for possible bodies and compared fingerprints against their files, all to no avail. Since it was too good a car to be discarded, they were sure it was hot but until the Demarest alarm came out, they had been without clues. Now they would forward the fingerprints for Fellows to check and their men would keep an eye out for the missing owner and his wife. It was possible they had friends there.

It was a possibility that Fellows regarded as faint. More likely George and Deirdre had left the empty car, taken the ferry back to Manhattan and dropped the license plates over the side. But if Staten Island's mystery was solved, Stockford's was deepened. Why Staten Island and why so soon? The Demarests could have put a whole day's driving behind them before the first alarm could have gone out. It made Fred Fellows wonder about their traveling south. Could they be hiding out in New York instead?

If the Stockford chief had a problem that noon, he was not alone. Television writer Stanley Somers discovered one of his own when he sat down to brunch with Dixie and Carl Randolph.

Though he'd been staying with them the week since he'd moved out of Jerry's house and out of her life, this was the first time he'd seen them since he'd gone in to New York Thursday morning. He'd been very late getting home the night before. A few of the people connected with the show had got together after the taping. There'd been a few drinks and some fooling around and they'd ended up at Jim Meyer's apartment, three men and two girls and one of the girls had been boozy enough to be willing and Stan was on the loose now and what the hell? She couldn't affect a man the way Deirdre did, but she was a cute kid all the same, even if she was too loaded to do more than be accommodating. Anyway, what with one thing and another, it was close to five A.M. before he got his car in Carl's garage and the key in the door.

Now, at noon, over scrambled eggs, fried chicken livers, whiskey sours and coffee, he was filled in by Carl and Dixie on recent events, the hunt for George, the probings by the police.

"That dumb jerk Fogarty," Stan growled. "Why didn't he keep his mouth shut?"

Dixie said, "He wants his money back, I reckon."

"Sure, and I'd like my money back too. So would we all. But not at the expense of our reputations. Can't you see it in all the scandal sheets and on the front page of the *Times*? 'Reputable citizens caught in bribe attempt.' Didn't he think about that?"

"I'm sure he did," Dixie answered. "But I don't suppose he thought that kind of publicity would hurt *his* reputation. I mean, it would be sort of expected of him, wouldn't it? Him being the kind of man he is and all?"

"Well it's going to give the rest of us a big black eye. It might even land us in jail."

Carl said, "So far all the papers have said is that George stole sixty thousand dollars and that Dan Fogarty made the complaint. The reporters have been after Dan, of course, but I talked to him. I laid it on the line to him and he'll keep mum from here on out. He's not telling the reporters anything. He won't even admit he lost money and he won't say who has. So right now the reporters don't know who was involved, how George got the money, or what it was for."

"For how long won't they know? If I were a newspaper editor, that's the first thing I'd be after."

Carl sat back and drummed his fingers on the table. "That's right and that's what they *are* after, and that's the point, This is information we don't want to come out. We don't want reporters knowing who we are."

"And how do we stop them from finding out?"

"There's a chance. The only people outside our own group who know are the police."

"And how long are they going to sit on that information?"

"Now don't get so upset, Stan. They haven't revealed it yet and there's every reason to believe they won't. After all, they have no evidence. I've talked to Dan and Mary and while they admitted to the police what the money was for in the beginning, they're ready to deny it now. I told the cops we were lobbying with it and Dan and Mary will back me up. That's the story all of us are to stick to from now on. There's going to be no more talk about bribery. So what can the cops say? Also, Warren told me he thinks the whole thing was a trick—that there isn't any Big Boy up in Hartford or anywhere else. Demarest made it all up. So, you see, there wasn't any bribery attempt after all."

"That's no good, Carl. Even if that's right, we had the intent."

"But my point is this. We didn't bribe anybody. And if we deny we ever intended to, the police could find themselves in real trouble if they accused us of it. They've got no proof. Not one shred of evidence. I think the police are going to be very careful not to say a word about bribery. If they do, we slap them with a lawsuit. Libel. Defamation of character. They won't dare open their mouths."

"Yeah," Somers said slowly. "I guess we're not so bad off after all."

"Not so long as we all stick to the same story."

Somers nodded. "O.K. That's better."

"Except for one thing."

Stan paused with his fork halfway to his mouth. Carl's measured words had ominous overtones. "Yeah? What?"

"One of our little group might not keep quiet."

Somers' eyes narrowed. "Who?"

"Jerry."

"Jerry? You mean you think she'd spill it to the cops?"

"Not the cops. She already has. Yesterday afternoon. She told them it was bribery—and in no uncertain language. But that's not what I'm thinking about. The cops won't say a word. They can't. I'm worried about her spilling it to the newspapers."

"Jerry? She's not that dumb."

"She's pretty mad at the lot of us. She's very bitter, Stan."

"Bitter?"

"About you leaving her. Warren thinks she'd like to get back at you."

"She wouldn't talk, Carl. *You* know why I left her. Because she wouldn't quit Warren. And I warned her. I said, 'Call it off, or we're through.' And she wouldn't. So if she wants him that much, she's not going to do anything against him."

"Things have changed, Stan. Warren's dropped her. He hasn't had anything to do with her since the weekend before George took the money. That's even before you left her."

"It may have been before I left her, but it was after I'd decided to."

"All right, but now you see, Jerry feels betrayed. She's not only bitter against you, she's very bitter against Warren. He told me so yesterday. And he said she's threatened to ruin us all. Apparently she hasn't yet, but I don't mind telling you, I was afraid to open the paper this morning. What I think we've got to do is cool her off fast."

"Yeah? How?"

Randolph coughed and glanced at Dixie. "Well, I was thinking—and Warren agrees. If you were to go back to her—"

"Oh. You and Warren, eh? You've got it all worked out how 'we' can fix it all up. Only you mean me! I'm the one who's got to do it."

"It would only be till this thing blows over."

"Forget it. She wouldn't have me back anyway. Not after I walked out."

"If you used the right approach—You know. You've been thinking it over—"

"You mean crawl to her? You mean she shacks up with Warren and I'm to beg forgiveness? I may be broadminded but—"

"Yes, but wait a minute, Stan. You're not exactly innocent. If you hadn't gone after Deirdre, she wouldn't have turned to Warren. You're partly to blame, you know."

Somers pushed his chair back. "Now just hold on. I didn't have any eyes on Deirdre in the beginning. I was a faithful husband. Three marriages and five damned long years of batching it? I'm forty-six and I'm tired of running around. When I married Jerry, I wanted it to be for keeps. I wanted to settle down and be comfortable. And I did my part. I was a faithful and devoted husband. Until we got into this big land deal. I wish to hell I'd never let you persuade me to buy up some of that property. Because that's when the trouble all started. All of a sudden we're thrown in with her ex-husband and the wife he'd left her for and that got her started. *She* was the one who was looking at Deirdre. Not me. She was the one who kept saying, 'How'd you like to go to bed with that?' She wanted me to. She wanted to put the knife into George. Even when it was obvious Warren was getting places with her, she still was egging me. So I began to notice. And I began to think. So Jerry was real sick? So she wants me to go after Deirdre? Well, that won't be any hardship at all. Why not?

"That's the way it started and she's the one who started it. So then she doesn't like it, is that my fault?"

Dixie said, "But Stan, honey, that's when you should have stopped."

"I couldn't stop. You don't turn those things on and off. The more I saw of Deirdre, the more I wanted to see of her. She does that to you."

Dixie said, "Even knowing what she was? Even knowing about Warren?"

"You close your eyes to it. And one thing about Deirdre. When you're with her, she makes you feel like the only man in the world.

"So Jerry started taking up with Warren. And she wasn't very subtle about it either. Neither of them were for that matter.

"I didn't object because I minded their going to bed together. I objected because it doesn't look good. She was doing to me what she'd got me to do to George. Well, I decided this girl is real sick and I wasn't going to stand for it. There's nothing there any more. No feeling. It's all gone. So don't try to tell me to go back to her. I don't want any part of her."

Carl nodded sympathetically. "I know what you mean, Stan. But don't think about it as going back to her. Think about it as playing a game."

"Let Warren play the game. Let him go back to her."

"That won't do. He's not her husband."

"So what? He'd keep her happier."

Dixie put a hand on his arm. "Stan, honey, what Carl means is the police don't know you've broken up. It's not going to do any good for them to find out. It's bad enough their knowing what the money was for. It'd be worse if they knew all the other things that were going on."

"Well, dammit," Stan said angrily, "why do they have to know anything? Why don't we call off the hunt for George. Let him have his goddam sixty thousand dollars. I'd be more than glad to take the loss just to be left alone."

"So would we," Dixie said. "So would Warren. Unfortunately, Dan and Mary don't seem to feel the same way. They want their money back."

"Aaah," Somers said in disgust. "Those money-grubbing bastards. All right, why don't we chip in and pay them back the money they lost?"

Carl said, "You mean nine thousand dollars?"

"Is that what it is? I thought it was less."

"Nine thousand. That would mean 'hree thousand from you, Warren and me." He frowned. "I don't know."

"Three thousand?" Somers groaned and said, "God damn."

"Can you raise three thousand?"

Somers groaned again. "I don't know that I could raise a hundred bucks. I'm mortgaged to the hilt. I had to sweat blood trying to raise the fifty-four hundred for George's little nest-egg. And now, with Jerry, there'll be alimony. God damn it. And I don't know how the show's going to go. We've only got a thirteen-week contract with options and if the ratings are bad, the network will drop it and, hell, I won't even have a job until my agent can line me up something else. I'm over a barrel."

Carl said, "I couldn't manage to stake you, Stan. I'm out twenty thousand already and I'm damned if I want to throw any more down the drain. And especially I don't like the idea of making up Fogarty's loss. Nobody's going to be making up mine."

"Maybe if I talked to Dan—"

"I don't know. I don't think Dan counts any more. Even if we all refused to press charges, I think it's out of our hands now. The papers say George's insurance company is all hot and bothered. They're going to want him caught even if we don't."

"Well, you can't expect me to go back to Jerry to shut her up. That wouldn't do any good, just living in the same house with her to fool the cops. That won't make her any less bitter."

"The idea, of course, would be to fool *her.*"

"Fat chance."

Dixie said gently, "You're a television writer, aren't you, Stan? And didn't Carl tell me you did some acting before you went into the writing end? Weren't you in some of those day-time serials? You could do it."

Somers put his head in his hands. "Oh, Jesus."

"You could do it, Stan. You could make her believe."

Somers looked up. "Listen, I could live in the same house with her. I could manage that. But you're suggesting a lot more. You want me to go through the whole bit."

Carl said, "Pretend she's Deirdre in the dark."

"Very funny. There's no similarity, dark or light."

"All right, but she's still a very attractive woman, Stan. That oughtn't to be so hard to take."

"The thought of kissing her makes me ill. God, isn't there some other way?"

Dixie said, "Not if we don't want her shooting off her mouth to the papers." She brought the phone over on a long extension cord and put it before him. "It can mean your job," she said. "She could kill you in television. And, knowing what she did to get back at George, you know she wouldn't hesitate, don't you?"

"No. She wouldn't hesitate." Somers stared at the phone bleakly, his shoulders bent. Finally, he lifted the receiver and dialed. There was a wait and then he swallowed and said, "Jerry? This is Stan."

13

The days of the following week produced little that was new to police headquarters on the Demarest case. Wilks talked to Stanley Somers and his wife on Tuesday but Stanley said nothing that hadn't been said before and very little that had.

On Wednesday there were reports from the Shoreham police on George's family and what his friends back home had to say. He had only been up there once since his remarriage and that was for Christmas in 1964. That visit and a visit his family made to Stockford comprised the only two times they had met his wife. They didn't even know of the wedding, performed by a justice of the peace, until after it had happened.

As for the suggestion that George stole sixty thousand dollars, they said it was not at all like George. He was not that kind of man and they were sure there was some mistake. If there were no mistake, then something extraordinary must have happened to George to make him change like that. They had no idea what that something might have been and they had no idea where he might have gone with the money. He certainly hadn't come to them.

By Friday the story was long out of the newspapers. The last item had appeared Monday and mentioned that the abandoned car had led the chief of police to suspect the fugitives were hiding out in New York. What George's parents had had to say didn't rate any space at all and after that there had been nothing.

As for the police in Stockford, their attention was on other things. There were traffic violations, there was a fight in a bar, there was a theft of copper tubing at a construction site. The case of George Demarest and the missing sixty thousand dollars wasn't mentioned any more. The alarm was out, the pictures had been circulated and until somebody, somewhere, reported a sighting there wasn't anything to be done.

But the case wasn't completely forgotten. When Wilks and Edwin Harris came in from a round of questioning regarding the copper tubing theft near noon on Friday, they found Fellows sitting somberly at the main desk staring into space. He came out of his brown study slowly and looked them over. "You making out?"

"We've got a couple of leads. A footprint we've made a plaster cast of and a name to be checked out."

"Where'd you get the name?"

"From one of the guys we talked to who we thought might be involved. He claims he wasn't but he thinks he knows who did it."

"You try the junkyards in the area to see if the stuff's turned up?"

"Not yet. We're going to try this guy first. If we can find him. He's not home right now."

Fellows nodded and Wilks told Harris he could get some lunch. "And bring some coffee back with you. How do you want yours, Fred?"

"Never mind me. I'm going out."

"Milk and sugar in mine," Wilks told the departing Harris and turned to the chief. "Anything important?"

"Carl Randolph is going to take me out and show me the hundred and eighty-eight acres the fuss was all about. Especially the part belonging to Demarest.

"What's he want to do that for?"

"I asked him to."

"Oh?" Wilks arched an eyebrow. "You think Demarest is hiding there or something?"

Fellows smiled faintly. "No. Hardly."

"Then why the interest? Why does his land matter? Why, in fact, does catching him matter? I don't think that gang of thieves wants him caught."

"That's not what's bothering me. I'm wondering what he's done."

"Done? He's stolen sixty thousand dollars. Or, at least,

that's what everybody says." Wilks eyed the chief suddenly.
"Why? Do you think otherwise?"

"No. I'm not questioning that. I'm just wondering if that's
all he's done. There's something funny. I didn't notice it at
the time, at least consciously, but it must have hit me sub-
consciously because I've had this vague uneasy feeling all
week. Then last night I had a dream and I dreamed I was
looking through Demarest's garage and then I remembered."

"Remembered what?"

"The tools he had there."

"What about them?"

Fellows smiled. "Remember what they were?"

Wilks reflected. "Rakes, shovel, lawn mower, and an ax. No
blood on the ax."

"That's right."

"And that disturbs you? Now if there *had* been blood on
the ax—"

"You missed it too. All right, what's the lawn mower for?
To mow his lawn with. The rakes? For leaves and things. He's
got some trees in the yard. The ax? Maybe to chop up dead
branches, right?"

"Right."

"So now, what would he use the shovel for?"

Wilks frowned and Fellows said, "That's right. There's no
garden. There're no plantings. There's nothing to dig."

"Maybe his wife was going to put in some plantings."

"Maybe, but the shovel had been used. It had already done
digging. The question is where?"

"And you think it's out on his property somewhere?"

"I think it's the obvious first place to look."

Wilks said, "Uhmmm," and rubbed his chin thoughtfully.
"And why would he be digging?" He looked at Fellows.
"Mind if I go along?"

14

Carl Randolph came by for Fellows and Wilks at quarter of
one in a blue-gray 1966 Cadillac. He was in jovial spirits this
afternoon, a willing cooperator with the police. After all,
things had worked out pretty well. There had been no bad
publicity about any bribery attempts—better yet, almost no

publicity at all. Jerry had been silenced and Stan had been got out of the house. (It wasn't that he didn't trust his cousin, or that he didn't trust Dixie, but it was awkward having a third person around, particularly one who worked at home most of the week.) Furthermore, members of the group had got together on their story and all of them, including the Fogartys, were willing to insist, should the subject come up, that the money had only been gathered to promote the idea of a super-highway in the area. He could almost believe, in fact, that they really were nothing more than a group of public-spirited citizens working for the common good, only to be grievously robbed by a foul conspirator who had taken advantage of their public generosity. On this day he didn't much mind the fact the police were still seeking George Demarest. Who knew but that they might even find him. Carl Randolph might even get some of his money back.

"So you want to see the land that caused all the trouble?" he asked when the policeman got into the car with him, Fellows in front, Wilks in back. "It's good land. It's cost us all a little more than we expected, thanks to dear George, and we aren't going to make the profit we thought we were when Persall took out the option, but we'll get our money back in time and a little extra to boot. It's going to be developed one of these days. Everything's going to get developed the way the population's going up. Land's the thing to sink your money into. You got any loose cash sitting around, don't stick it in the bank. Put it in real estate. I've got some nice pieces I can show you. A lot of the farmers around are willing to let go a little of their acreage. But you better buy soon. The price goes up every year."

Fellows said, "Is that why Somers bought?"

"Yeah. I persuaded him. I saw that section. Belonged to a farmer and when he died, the family wanted to get rid of it. That was back in '60, but they wanted three hundred and nobody would go that high. A couple of years later, though, three hundred wasn't a bad price. That's when Demarest bought up his forty-four acres. The next year Wilcox bought thirty-six. I would've got in back then myself but my money was tied up in another enterprise. In '64, I had the money but the price had gone up to five hundred. It was worth it even so and I bought as much of it as I could and persuaded Stan to buy what he could. The Fogartys took what was left the next year."

He swung onto Center Street and headed east. "You fellas interested in buying some land? I always say, diamonds may be a girl's best friend, but land is a man's. You own land, you can never starve. You can always raise food. And you've got a place to live."

Fellows laughed shortly. "We're policemen, not television writers or psychiatrists or insurance salesmen. We don't have that kind of money."

"Doesn't take much. Five hundred dollars for an acre most places. I can get you half an acre some places for three hundred."

Wilks said, "We could maybe manage a cupful of soil."

"I know you guys. You're socking it away in the bank. You're making a mistake. You take my wife. Her first husband left her pretty well fixed when he died. And she invested in land. She's got quite a lot down in South Carolina and she's bought some up here. She's a shrewd businesswoman, Dixie is."

Fellows said, "She was married before?"

"Down in Charleston. It was very tragic. Her husband and son were killed in a plane crash in 1958. He had his own plane. Used it for business and pleasure. He was taking the boy for a ride. The boy was eight. Anyway, she and her daughter, who was seven at the time, came north and she worked in an advertising agency for a while. I met her at a party Stan had and we got married in 1960."

"Your first marriage?"

Randolph laughed. "Hell, no. I've been through the mill. I got married the first time back in '44. One of those wartime things. You're in the Army, you may never come back—that sort of stuff. We had two quick children and six years of finding out we didn't belong together before we called it quits. They live on the West Coast now. The kids come east once a year. Then I made another mistake ten years later, in 1954, but it only took two years to cancel that one out. I thought I was through with marriage after that, until Dixie came along. The other two were flibberty-gibbets but Dixie's got a real head on her shoulders. As a matter of fact, she handles all my books. Does it better than I."

They drove out Center and picked up East Street, traveling east. Randolph said, "You think you'll ever catch George and Deirdre?"

"It's not unlikely—eventually."

"With a country this big to hide in I don't know how you could ever expect to do it."

"It's not as big as it looks. Or rather, it's big but people don't hide in much of it."

"Yeah? What do you mean?"

"You belong in a certain class of society. Wherever you

go you gravitate to that class. Wherever the Demarests go we can expect they'll move in the same kind of circle they moved in here."

Randolph said, "Better circles if he can con people into thinking he's better. He was always trying to look like he belonged higher up than he did."

"That's something to remember."

The property was way out Long Mountain Road near Vesper Road in the northeast corner of Stockford. It was a large wooded area, rolling and sloping slightly but, for the most part, flat. Its boundaries were natural ones, rock ledges and cliffs, marsh lands and the two roads. It was a quiet, untouched area, bright with turning leaves against a deep blue sky.

"There you are." Randolph said. "Looks pretty, doesn't it?"

"Umhmm," Fellows said. "Who owns which parts?"

"Well, I should've brought a map. You'd get a better idea. You wouldn't even need to come out here. Demarest own this part bordering the road and back in a ways. You see that dirt road on the right? Wilcox owns from there to the ledge up ahead. Thirty-six acres. My section and Stan's is back of theirs and Fogarty's got the end piece back of us bordering the marsh."

"Any way to get to those properties?"

"That roadway we just passed. That's a right of way through to the land in back. The West family, who originally owned it, had that put in when they sold off the front pieces."

"Can you take us in on it?"

Randolph slowed the car. "You want to go in there? I thought you just wanted to see where the property was."

"I'd like to see where the different sections are."

"It's all pretty much the same. Undeveloped woodland with a couple of right of ways going through. You can't really call them roads. The Wests just had a bulldozer plow a path between the trees and around the rocks. There's nothing to see in there you can't see from the outside. I can show you on a map."

"You don't want to take us in?"

"Well, sure if you want." Randolph wasn't happy about it. "This is a new Cadillac. I'd have to go pretty slow."

"That's all right, I want to go slowly."

"S'up to you." Randolph stopped the car, backed around and returned to the little dirt road that entered the property, swung in and crawled ahead. A few yards of fill marked the start of it but that quickly ended and thereafter only stony ruts showed the way and sometimes these almost disappeared leaving only space between trees to indicate the path. It was bumpy in spots, often tilted, and as the car wound through, it sometimes heeled well over. Randolph said, "If I'd known you wanted to go in, I'd've brought the station wagon. I've never driven the Cadillac in here before."

"Are there any other roads and trails in here besides this one?"

"Not in Demarest's or Wilcox's property. They never touched it. I had a bulldozer blaze a few trails through mine and I guess Fogarty did too. So we could get through and see what we had and what we could do with it. Why? Are you going to want to go on those too? They aren't even as well marked as this."

"I'd like to see everything if I may."

"I don't get what you're looking for."

"Let's say I want a complete understanding of all the ins and outs of the place."

"O.K., but I'm damned if I know how that's going to help you find George."

The trail branched left and right and Randolph went left. "I'll show you my land first. Stan doesn't have any trails on his. Then we'll go back and see what Fogarty's got."

"You been up here recently? Over these trails?"

"I haven't been up here since I showed the Persall people around."

They bumped slowly over the ground till they reached the base of the rock ledge in a small field and Randolph backed around. "Demarest property on this side, mine on that." He started back and made a turn off into his property at a hardly noticeable spot. Fellows said, "A little oil on some of this grass we're going over."

"Yeah."

"Sure you haven't been up here?"

"No. Maybe somebody else has."

They eased up a shallow rise, did a sharp turn around a tree and passed a gurgling brook. They twisted on a zigzag pattern, heard the rippling of the brook again, and rounded a sharp bend. On the right as they straightened was a small open patch of sparse grass and soft soil among the thin trees and scraggly bushes. Near the back of it, twenty yards off the trail, dead leaves and branches were collected, covering a small patch of ground.

Fellows told Randolph to stop. He pointed. "What about that, Sid?"

"That looks man-made."

"That's what I think."

71

The two men got out simultaneously and Randolph, puzzled, slid across the seat and followed. "I don't get it," he said. "I don't know what the devil you're looking for."

Fellows extended an arm. "Hold it now, Mr. Randolph. Don't go wandering off there just yet. You stay behind us." The chief started forward slowly, side by side with Wilks.

Randolph, frowning, looked around at the ground as the policemen were doing and tried to fathom what they expected to find.

"There," Wilks said and pointed to a soft spot in the ground. "Tire marks."

"Right. Keep away from those, Mr. Randolph."

They detoured around the impressions and found another trace that rain had all but obliterated. They approached the gathered leaves and Fellows spotted a glasses case lying in the dirt among tufts of dry grass a few feet to the left. "There's something."

"Here's something else." Wilks stopped the chief and pointed to the edge of the collected covering of leaves. It was the rainwashed but still distinct impression of a woman's stylish shoe.

Randolph said, "By golly, that's a woman's footprint! There's been a woman up here."

"She's no hiker," Wilks said. "Not in pumps like that."

"Don't go near it, Mr. Randolph." Fellows went over to the glasses case. It was of dark brown leather, stiffened by weather, with black hornrims protruding. He crouched and studied it for a bit, then lifted it by the edges, looked at the other side and called the real estate man. "Don't touch it, just look at it, Mr. Randolph. Initials GRD. You ever see this before?"

"My God, he said. "Those are George's."

"Demarest wore glasses?"

"For reading. What the hell are they doing out here?"

"That promises to be a very interesting question." Fellows repositioned the case exactly as he had found it, initialed side down, and got to his feet. "Sid," he said, "I don't think anybody will be coming around before I get back but I guess you'd better stay anyway. I'll make it as soon as I can. All right, Mr. Randolph. We can go now. Sorry to have taken so much of your time."

They returned to the car, Randolph glancing back at the impassive Wilks who had propped a foot on a dead log and was biting off a chew of tobacco. "I just don't get it," Randolph said as he started up. "I think you expected to find those glasses there. How did you know he'd lost his glasses?

And how did you know where they were?"

"I didn't. Please don't turn around in there. It might mess up things."

"Sure. Whatever you say." He drove on ahead. "You think George and Deirdre buried something there? The money?"

"Maybe. Maybe not. We're going to find out."

15

For Carleton Randolph it was all very exciting. Fellows seemed more than willing to have him tag along and he was glad to be a witness to matters. He had never watched the police on a case before and he was intensely curious as to what had been buried on his property. He was sure it wasn't money now. There was something else in the ground, perhaps a body. Would the chief be calling in a photographer, would he be summoning two of the squad cars and making arrangements with the man on the desk about the four o'clock shift for anything less?

The photographer was a man named Hank Lemmon, Randolph found, and he rode back to the spot with them. They went, this time, in the chief's car because it had a two-way radio and the chief wanted to do the driving.

They arrived back at the spot at quarter after three and Wilks showed them two more places where he'd found tire marks. The car or whatever it was had apparently backed off the trail in among the trees to where the digging had taken place. Fellows noted the spots and had Lemmon take pictures, the chief laying a ruler alongside the marks.

Two policemen came out in a following squad car. They propped a couple of shovels against a fender and were set to work by Fellows going over the ground in all directions looking for other things besides the glasses that might have been dropped.

Wilks made a plaster of Paris solution from materials the chief had in his trunk and, after Lemmon was through with his pictures, he sprayed the tire marks and footprint and poured the plaster of Paris into them.

Fellows and Wilks began uncovering an area where it was obvious the ground had been dug up, replaced and trampled down. "I just can't understand why George would leave his glasses here," said Randolph.

Wilks said, "He laid his coat down to dig. They fell out when he picked it up."

"Wouldn't he notice?"

"Not at night. And this was done at night."

"How do you know?"

"He would have done a better job of disguising this place if he could have seen what he was doing."

Fellows, removing more leaves and branches, said, "He's trampled this thing down but he hasn't left any footprints. Only these impressions here." He indicated overlapping marks roughly rectangular with fuzzy, uncertain edges. "You know what I bet he did, Sid? Wrapped cardboard around his shoes."

"He knew where he was going to dig. He had this spot picked out beforehand."

"He may have done the digging in advance too. Hey, Hank, you want to get a picture of these marks when we get it cleared?"

Patrolman Zolton Chernoff, hunting through the brush a good fifty yards off and across the roadway, called out, "I found this!" He held up a hunk of corrugated cardboard. "There're two of them."

"You got something," Fellows called back. "Keep looking."

He and Wilks finished exposing the trampled area, casting the leaves and branches to one side. The chief went back to the car for a large reel tape measure and, with Wilks' help, stretched the flexible steel ribbon lengthwise over the trampled spot. "About eight and a half to this point," he said and they walked around to get the width. "Four here. Maybe a little more." He cranked in the tape, made a note on his pad and had Lemmon take a final photograph. He called to the patrolmen. "Hey, Chernoff, Kettleman. You find anything else?"

They hadn't and he said, "Mark your spots and bring over the shovels. We're ready."

The patrolmen brought over the shovels and Chernoff looked at the large rectangle with narrowed eyes. "So it's like that, huh?"

"It's like that," Fellows said. "Start in the middle."

Kettleman dug in his shovel and threw his dirt toward the nearby stream. Chernoff widened the hole.

Wilks said to Fellows, "When did it rain last? I can't remember."

"There was a rainy day last week. And the day before Labor Day it poured."

"Oh, yes. That was my day off. How'd you remember?"

"Harris remembered. I asked him back at headquarters."

74

Chernoff and Kettleman went down a foot and a half and widened the hole some more. Kettleman pushed his shovel a couple of inches deeper and stopped. "I've hit something."

Wilks, Fellows and Randolph moved closer and Chernoff turned his shovel and started scraping the dirt carefully. A patch of blue and white polka-dot material came into view. Randolph started and said in horror, "Oh, my God! It's Deirdre!"

Fellows turned to watch him. "How do you know it's Deirdre?"

"That's the dress she was wearing that last night."

Chernoff and Kettleman, digging carefully, uncovered the rest of the skirt and then, below that, the moldering remains of a human knee. Fellows waited for that and then, without a word, walked back to his car. He got into the side seat, picked up the mike and said, "Unger from Fellows. Did Harris tell you?"

"Yes. We're standing by."

"All right. It's a body. Lemmon's here so it's just Mac-Farlane and the ambulance we want. Long Mountain Road, short of Vesper. I'll have a squad car meet them."

"Long Mountain. Right."

"And tell the press."

"You want the press?"

"We've got a real hunt on our hands now. I'm going to want all the publicity I can get."

16

C. W. Lawrence, editor of the *Stockford Weekly Bulletin,* was the first member of the press to arrive. He maneuvered to a halt and got out, following by five minutes the ambulance and Medical Examiner James MacFarlane. Hank Lemmon briefed him and he joined MacFarlane and Fellows at the grave site. Most of the eight and a half by four foot area had been excavated in a search for anything else that might have been buried and the mortal remains of Deirdre Demarest lay dirty, rotting and exposed in its center. The bosom of her polka-dot dress was bloodstained and there was a small hole in it over her heart. Lawrence, looking once and looking away, said to MacFarlane, "Shot to death, Jim?"

MacFarlane, old and weary and heavy, said, "Looks that way. An autopsy will tell." He gestured to the two-man ambulance crew and said, "Take her out now." He didn't wait but started back and Fellows walked with him, one hand guiding the old man gently where the footing was uneven. "Got a cold," MacFarlane mumbled. "I'm going to sit in the car."

"Can you give me an offhand figure on how long she's been dead? Three weeks be about right?"

"As long as you recognize it's offhand, I'd say about three weeks."

Four more reporters, driven in a squad car by Harvey Cassidy, arrived as the ambulance attendants were lifting the sheet-covered body, strapped to the stretcher, into the back of the ambulance. One was Richard Harrington, reporter for the *Pittsfield Chronicle,* two were from the wire services and one was a television newscaster from Pittsfield. Fellows showed them the grave and the tire and footmarks from which the casts had been removed and he said the girl had apparently been shot.

The ambulance backed in and turned around and Fellows paused to wave to MacFarlane. Randolph joined them and Fellows introduced him as the owner of the property.

"Know who she is yet, Chief?" one newsman asked.

"Deirdre Demarest. Remember the story I gave you about the couple who ran off with sixty thousand dollars? George and Deirdre Demarest? Well, the identity of the couple has changed a little. It's George and some other woman now. And they did more than run off with some money. They killed and buried his wife."

The reporters made noises and wrote rapidly for a bit and paused. "How'd you come to find her?"

Fellows explained about the shovel and the puzzle over where it had been used. "Demarest owns property up here so I got Mr. Randolph to show me around the places a car could go. We found it had been used here."

"You suspected it had been used to bury a body, didn't you? Why?"

Fellows scratched his chin. "Well, now I guess you've got me. It's hard to say. It was a kind of feeling, I guess. You see, in asking around about George and Deirdre we got stories that neither one of them was faithful to the other. In fact, one of the reasons advanced for George running off with the money was to get his wife away from men she'd been seeing around here. That was a possibility, of course, but it seemed more likely to me that a guy with sixty thousand dollars and an unfaithful wife would be more likely to run off without her than with her. Particularly if he was playing around too. And if he was, why should she want to go with him? I suppose, in the back of my mind, I was wondering if they really had gone off together as everybody thought or whether only one had gone. I think that's why I wanted to know what the shovel had been used for."

"Any ideas on who the other woman is who he ran off with?"

"Not much yet. We tried one of the dead woman's shoes in the footprint after we removed the cast and it's much too small. Mrs. Demarest was only about five foot three. From the size of the print we'd guess the woman who made it was from five six to five eight."

"Any women reported missing around here?"

Fellows shook his head.

"Could that mean the woman is from somewhere else?"

"Not necessarily. Women can go away without having it reported to the police. They move all the time, get jobs somewhere else, get married—or say they have."

"Got any theories, Chief? What do you think happened."

Fellows said, "My guess is he killed her the night he got the money and he and the other woman brought her up here in the dark and buried her. Probably used the station wagon he's got. We'll be checking the tires when we go back. Then the two of them took off in the Thunderbird he owned."

"Why night? Why do you think they did it at night?"

"The glasses case for one thing. It apparently fell out of his jacket when he laid it down to do the shoveling. He would have spotted it in the daytime. Also, I don't think the woman would have left a footprint in the daytime. And then there's the way the burial spot was concealed. They gathered leaves and branches from all around to hide the spot but the concentration of all the leaves and debris on that one patch of ground called attention to it instead. They would have noticed that in the daytime. They would have done a better job of disguising the grave."

"Yeah, but to go out and dig a grave in the middle of the night—"

"We think it was already dug, the spot picked, the hole made. It's too good a choice. The ground's soft and easy to work with. Also the grave is larger than necessary, and deeper. It was plenty roomy. That shows it wasn't any rush job. If you've got the body with you, you're going to make a hole only barely big enough to fit her in and cover her over. We have to conclude the hole was ready and all they did was put

77

the girl into it, fill it up, stamp it down and cover it over."

Harrington said, "That's supposition, Chief. What about the danger of leaving an exposed hole? Suppose somebody came along?"

"Not much likelihood, not way in here. It should be worth the gamble. At worst the body might be discovered, but maybe not till we couldn't identify it. At best, of course, it would never be found and he'd have people looking for him and his wife, not the kind of woman he's with."

"Who identified the body?"

"Mr. Randolph here."

That interested the reporters. They turned. "You knew Mrs. Demarest?"

Randolph didn't welcome Fellows' disclosure. He didn't want to be in this at all. "Well, yes," he admitted reluctantly and added by way of explanation, "The Demarests had the property in front of mine."

"How well did you know them?"

Randolph glanced nervously at the chief's impassive face. Would Fellows understand that it was necessary to lie? The chief seemed like a decent sort. After all he hadn't spilled the story yet. Maybe he wouldn't now. "Not very well," Randolph said to the reporters. "We were only acquaintances."

Harrington's eyes narrowed. He was brusque and often offensive, but he could smell a story. He broke in. "Did you know anything about the murder, Mr. Randolph? Did you suspect Demarest had killed his wife?"

"No, no. It never occurred to me. It was the chief's idea. He's the one who wanted me to show him around." Randolph laughed a little. "I didn't have the faintest idea what he was looking for."

"This comes as a shock, then?"

"Oh, yes. A great shock."

"You knew he'd run off with sixty thousand dollars?"

This was the critical point. He prayed Fellows wouldn't give him away. "No," he said. "No, I didn't know anything about that."

Harrington feigned surprise. "You mean the chief didn't tell you? You didn't see it in the papers?"

Fellows hadn't flickered an eyelash and Randolph felt emboldened. "No. I didn't know anything about it."

"You didn't know the chief was looking for Demarest? You knew him but you didn't know that? The chief never asked you about Demarest and where he might have gone?"

Randolph lost his boldness and began to perspire. Fellows might let him lie about his own actions but he knew the chief wouldn't sit still for any lies about the police. "Well, now that I think of it, I recall a policeman was around asking about George. I think he did mention something about George having gone off with some money."

A wolfish gleam appeared in Harrington's eye. He had his man now. He said, "You just happen to remember—now that I mention it—that a friend of yours stole some money? Is that what you're trying to tell us, Mr. Randolph?"

Randolph moistened his lips. "I never believe in judging a man. A man is innocent until proven guilty."

"That's not what I asked you, Mr. Randolph. I asked you if you wanted us to believe that you forgot the police were looking for him on a charge of theft."

"No, I just—didn't—uh—think I ought to comment on that. George was my friend."

Another reporter jumped in. "Did any of that money belong to you?"

Randolph turned. "Money? You mean the money—"

It was Harrington's turn. "The money he's accused of stealing. We don't want to judge him guilty. Let's say the money he allegedly stole?"

Randolph turned back, confused. "That money? Well, no. I don't know anything about the money."

"Then why did the police question you? Wasn't it because he'd taken the money from you?"

"No. He took the money from Fogarty."

"Your memory's getting better all the time," Harrington said sarcastically. "But if Demarest didn't steal money from you, why did the police talk to you?"

"Well, they wanted to know where I thought he might have gone or why he might have taken it."

"Why did they think you'd know?"

"I knew George—a little."

"You must have known him pretty well if the police expected you to know things like that about him. How well *did* you know him, Mr. Randolph?"

Randolph said desperately, "Look, you've got the wrong idea. George stole some money—"

"I thought you thought he was innocent."

"I mean it was alleged that he stole some money. The police talked to a lot of people. Not just to the people he stole the money from but other people who knew George."

All the reporters jumped on that one. "Oh, so he stole from more than one person?" Pencils flew and Harrington said, "I thought you didn't know anything about it."

"That's only my understanding of the matter. I mean that's what the police told me."

"You mean the police told you, but they wouldn't tell us?" Harrington and the others turned to Fellows.

The chief said quietly, "I think you all know me well enough so that I don't have to comment on that."

Harrington went to Randolph again. "What're you holding back? How many people did he steal the money from?"

"I don't know. Four or five, I guess."

"What're their names?"

"I wouldn't know who they are."

"Won't know or won't tell? Why is it a secret?"

"I don't know. They probably don't want publicity."

"They've been robbed and they don't want anybody to know it? Is that what you're trying to tell us?"

"Well, sometimes people don't want to publicize things like that."

"If you were robbed you'd want it publicized, wouldn't you?"

"No. Not necessarily."

"Is that why you're denying you were one of the people he robbed?"

Randolph tried to rally himself. He attempted a stiff, stern tone. "Listen, I'm just a bystander in all this. All I was doing was my civic duty, helping the police. I'm not going to answer any more questions. That's the chief's job."

"What kind of a scheme did Demarest use to get the money? Did it have anything to do with his property?"

"No."

"What, then?"

"I don't know."

"Then you *don't* know that it didn't have anything to do with his property."

"Well, I wouldn't think it would."

"Why?"

"I don't know."

"How many other people own property around here?"

"I don't know."

"You mean you know the Demarests because they own property here—know them well enough for the police to think you can help find them—but you don't know any of the other people who own property?"

"I hardly know them."

"Hardly? But you do know them?"

"Yes. I think I've met them."

"How many are there?"

"Owning property around here? What properties?"

"This whole woods. How many people own the woods?"

"Oh, I guess five, counting the Demarests."

"And he fleeced four or five people, did you say?"

"It didn't have to do with real estate, I tell you. It doesn't have anything to do with this property."

"You said you didn't know that it didn't, Mr. Randolph. What are the names of the other property owners?"

"Listen, I'm not going to be badgered. I said I wasn't going to answer any more questions."

"Surely you can tell us their names, Mr. Randolph."

"No, I said."

"We can find out at the town clerk's office. Why are you trying to hide their names from us, Mr. Randolph?"

"I said I'm not going to answer any more questions. You can get your answers from the chief. I've got to get back." He turned to Fellows. "I'm going to wait in the car." He stalked off rapidly and stumbled twice on the way.

17

The story of Deirdre Demarest's murder was the big news in Saturday's papers. Reporters, after a busy afternoon following Fred Fellows around, pieced together a story of lust and greed that had transformed a mild and friendly insurance agent into a thief and murderer.

When Fellows had got rid of the reporters, he settled down in his office with Wilks to discuss angles he had been considering. "The gun he used was a rifle of course," he said. "We don't have any applications from Demarest or anybody else in that crowd for pistol permits so unless he stole one somewhere—"

"Which he'd never do when you can get a rifle at any hardware or sporting goods store and who's to know?"

Fellows shrugged. "We'll have to see if somebody can tell us. Some stores dealing with guns will record your name if you buy a rifle. Others might remember who you were."

"If you buy it locally. Which I'm sure he wouldn't do. And there're the mail order houses."

"We'll have to make a check of stores anyway. We've got to try to trace the rifle to him if we want to build a case."

"Well, if he's in it with a woman, that'll make finding him easier. I hope."

"And if we can figure out where he might go, that'll make it easier yet."

"Let's see. He's got a suitcase full of cash. The question is, how long is he going to want to carry that around with him?"

"That's one point," Fellows agreed. "If he loses that suitcase, he's dead."

"Or if his girl-friend should run out on him and take it with her." Wilks picked up the plaster cast of the footprint that had been lying on the table with the tire casts. He studied it and shook his head. "I wish that damned drought had lasted a little longer. That hard rain the day before Labor Day sure didn't do this footprint any good. I can't pin it down closer than a $7\frac{1}{2}$ to $8\frac{1}{2}$, widths B to D. That's too big for Deirdre but it'll fit an awful lot of other girls. It's going to be no cinch finding our Cinderella."

"We're going to have to talk to a lot of people. Say, I just thought of something. Staten Island isn't the end of the world, is it? I mean it's not a cul-de-sac. Don't they have bridges from there to New Jersey?"

"I'm pretty sure they do. Yeah, of course they do."

Fellows snapped his fingers. "I think that's it, then. We've been thinking—or at least I have—that he left the car there to come back to New York and get a train out. But that raises some questions. As you said about the suitcase, he can't afford to lose it. That means he's not going to be awfully keen about throwing it up on the luggage rack of a railroad coach. He's going to want to keep that suitcase away from people."

"At least until he can convert that cash into something else."

"And that'll take time. And since he's guilty of murder and not just theft, he's got to be very careful. Therefore, the question is, if he wasn't planning to take a train, why did he abandon the car so close to home? He could have gone a thousand miles in it before any alarm."

"Like you say, he planned to hide out in New York."

"But he only took his summer clothes with him. That's the catch there. And there's only his fingerprints in the Thunderbird. That's the other catch."

"So maybe his lady-friend had a car of her own and that's the one they're using."

"And that, Sid is the answer. I'll lay odds on it. I didn't think of that until just now because I didn't realize Staten Island could be a route out—a route west. Now it makes sense. He takes his car to make it appear he and Deirdre have fled, abandons it across a state line without plates to make it

82

hard to trace, is picked up by the girl, and off they go."

"Which means our job is to find out who the girl is."

"That's the first order of business."

Wilks sat back and chewed his pencil for a bit. "And the best way to find out is to see if she left fingerprints in his house. That means I'm going to want prints of all the people in that gang to match with the unidentifieds Ed found there. Then we see what we've got left."

"And while you're getting their prints, ask them for everything they can tell you about the night of August twenty-fourth. When did they arrive? How did George behave? Deirdre? When did they leave and in what order? What did they see? You know the bit."

"Also the name of every woman anybody ever saw George look at."

"That's right, and meanwhile, don't forget to keep your fingers crossed that someone makes the job easy for us and phones in a tip."

18

No tips came in on Sunday or Monday to make the job easier and Sidney Wilks worked long and hard. Sunday he finger-printed and exhaustively interviewed the Fogartys, Somerses, Wilcoxes and Randolphs. Monday morning he turned over the prints to Ed Lewis for checking and gave Fellows a report. None of the eight people could name a woman George Demarest had shown any interest in. Of the eight, only Jerry Somers thought he played around at all. Her views, however, didn't impress the detective lieutenant. "She's in the best position to know," he admitted, "but I'm not eager to believe her."

"Why?" Fellows asked.

"If he was really like that, it seems to me the others would spot it. Also, she's got too much to gain by making such a claim. She shows up better if George deserted her because he was a chaser, than if he was a faithful husband who went off the deep end over another woman."

"Except," Fellows reminded him, "if he did go off the deep end for Deirdre, it wasn't long before he went off the deep end over another woman. And I don't think guys keep going off the deep end over somebody."

"Yeah, but wouldn't it show up to the others? A chaser can't hide the fact he's a chaser. He usually doesn't even want to."

"Sure, but those people were primarily business acquaintances. And his wife was there and his ex-wife. Before we draw any conclusions about George and women, I'd like to hear what some of the guys he knows at the country club have to say."

Wilks sighed. "I know. That's my job for today. Manny turned up five who knew him pretty well. I'm going to hunt them down and see if they give me a different picture."

"Let's hope they can give you some names."

As for the night of the pay-off which, by all the evidence, was the night of the murder, nothing, to the four couples, seemed out of the ordinary. George was, perhaps, more nervous than usual, but they put that down to his being responsible for all that money or, on hindsight, to getting his hands on it. Deirdre had been quiet and withdrawn as was her custom, pouring drinks and keeping in the background. She appeared totally unaware that she had only a few more hours to live.

All in the group were agreed on the facts of the evening. The Randolphs arrived first, at seven-thirty, having stopped at a drugstore for some allergy pills for Dixie. The Fogartys were last to leave, saying their goodbyes on the doorstep at nine o'clock as the Somerses backed out the drive. None had seen anyone hanging around, none remembered strange cars, none went near the house again that night.

"The Somerses and Randolphs went right home," Wilks said. "Somers had to work on a TV script most of the night down in his cellar. Wilcox took his wife home and went to his office to finish up some book he was writing. Fogarty dropped his wife and went to his office to work up a bid on a road construction job."

If Wilks could uncover no evidence as to the identity of the mysterious Madame X in the case, neither could Detective Sergeant Edward Lewis. He reported to Fellows later that morning that he had matched up all the unidentified fingerprints in the house and they all belonged to members of the group. Fogarty's were found on some of the furniture in the living room. One of Jerry Somers' was found in George's den, three more in the kitchen. Warren Wilcox had some time or other left four prints in the bedroom as well as six in more legitimate places. Dixie Randolph's were in the kitchen and Moira Wilcox's under the coffee table. No prints were found belonging to Carl Randolph, Mary Fogarty or Stan Somers. All the rest were Deirdre's and George's.

After Lewis had dispatched this bad news, it was Medical Examiner Jim MacFarlane's turn to come in. He arrived at noon with the autopsy protocol and brushed aside reporters until he had talked with the chief. He had a present to deliver too, he said, and shook it out of an envelope into Fellows' big hand. It was a smashed and battered bullet.

"That's the baby that did it," he said. "Twenty-two long rifle. It was lodged against the spine, having passed through the sternum and heart. I suppose you'll want the State Police ballistics people to look at it?"

"That's routine." Fellows examined it briefly and put it in another envelope and marked it. "Twenty-two rifle," he said. "That's what I expected. Kill her fast?"

"Death was instantaneous."

"Powder burns?"

"No. No burns. Here's the autopsy protocol. It's all in there, the bullet's path, the damage done, estimated time of death."

"Which was when?"

"Three to four weeks ago."

"What about identity?"

"You mean the girl? She's Deirdre Demarest all right. In addition to that fellow Randolph, we got an identification by her father. He came down from New London."

Fellows unfolded the autopsy protocol and skimmed it. "You checked her teeth, I see."

"That's right. And her dental record is attached. It's not my business to be a detective, but I thought you'd like the record. To my unofficial eye they match."

"Unofficial, my foot. O.K., Jim, and thanks."

"You want me to talk to those reporters outside?"

"You'd better. They're crying for stories and we don't have any."

"You're just sitting on your hands, I suppose?"

"We're trying to find the woman who left the footprint but we haven't made any progress so far."

MacFarlane wheezed heavily. "Whoever she is, she'll be trouble for Demarest."

"Is that official or unofficial?"

"That's official. Any woman who, even if she didn't help, would watch a man dispose of a woman he murdered, can't be anything but trouble."

In the afternoon two more visitors came into Fellows' office. The first was a perspiring Robert Armbruster who carried three long drawers stocked with 3″ x 5″ file cards. He put them down on the table in the main room long enough to tell reporters that Northeastern Insurance had obtained a court order giving them access to Demarest's office and accountants would start going over his books the next morning to see how much insurance money the fugitive agent had stolen. Then he lugged the drawers into Fellows' office and set them on the table there. "I thought you might want these," he said.

"What are they?"

"Demarest's files. These two," he said, putting his hands on a pair that were filled with cards, "are the names of people he's made calls on and the dates of each call. He indicated the third drawer, which was not quite a quarter full. "And these are cards on all the people he's sold insurance to. He's got it arranged by months. You see? So he'll know when to renew them."

"I see," Fellows said, observing the labels. "Three or four hundred customers, I'd guess. What do you have in mind?"

"Well, these are people who know George. They do business with him. Maybe someone in here knows where he is."

"And the other two drawers? There must be thirty-five hundred to four thousand cards in there."

"Well you never can tell what some of them might know. I want to do everything I can to help you find him and I thought maybe you might get something out of these files. At least I didn't think it would hurt to bring them to you."

Fellows laughed. "That's very thoughtful of you, Mr. Armbruster."

"That's all right. I want to help all I can. And as soon as our accountants go over everything, I'll let you know how much he stole."

"Thanks. I'll appreciate that too." Fellows watched the man leave, idly picked out some random cards from one of the drawers, frowned at them for a moment, then got out a pad of paper and pencil and sat down with the boxes.

The other visitor was County Coroner Clement Avery. He came in in midafternoon, and, after a short conference, announced to the members of the press that the inquest would be held Thursday afternoon in the town hall courtroom.

Wilks returned at quarter past seven as Fellows opened his office door and came out. "You didn't get anything?"

Wilks said, "Good night, are you still here?" He sighed. "No, nothing. I tracked them all down, all five of those club members who're supposed to know George so well, and they not only never heard about any woman, they're surprised to

86

learn there is one. I don't think he's got a girl-friend at all. I think it's a ghost-friend."

"Anyway we've got one lead. Came in this afternoon."

"What's that?"

"A bank clerk in Tulsa has identified Demarest as the man who robbed his bank this morning."

"Three cheers."

Fellows said, "Come in and have a hot cup of coffee. It'll make you feel better."

Wilks followed Fellows into the office and stopped when he saw the file drawers on the table. "What the hell are those?"

"Armbruster brought them over from Demarest's office."

Wilks picked out a card for a quick scan. "So, great. What are they?"

"All the people Demarest sells insurance to in that drawer. All the calls he's ever made in the others. Nine years' worth."

"Nice guy, that Armbruster. What does he want us to do with them?"

"Check them out."

"How many thousand names does he have here?"

"Probably around four. The only names that count would be those he contacted after his marriage to Deirdre. So it's only the last two years we have to concern ourselves with." He picked up a pad from atop the clutter on his desk. "I've been drawing up a list. It's not so many, actually. Forty-three who buy insurance from him and seventy-eight contacts he's made."

"Not so many? That's a hundred and twenty-one people to question about women in George's life."

"These are only the *women* he's seen about insurance since his marriage, not the men. I thought by this time, with all the publicity, we'd get a tip if some girl left town. We haven't, but that doesn't mean no girl has left. It merely means we haven't heard about it. My guess is that a girl is missing and her name is on that pad."

"We'll get busy tomorrow finding out. Unfortunately, even if you're right, that's only half the battle. *Who* she is won't tell us *where* she is."

"It might lead us to somebody who can."

19

On the back page of Wednesday's *Pittsfield Chronicle*, the evening paper most of Stockford read, was mention of the fact that twenty-eight years ago, on Wednesday, September 21, 1938, the great hurricane had struck. And on the front page this Wednesday, September 21, was a story that brewed its own storm. A two-column head read, MURDER SUSPECT SWINDLED FRIENDS IN LAND DEAL, and the story started, "George Demarest, Stockford insurance agent, sought by police in the murder of his wife, swindled four friends of $60,000 before fleeing town with another woman. Victimized by Demarest in a real estate deal were Carleton Randolph, wealthy real estate agent, Dr. Warren Wilcox, prominent psychiatrist, Stanley Somers, television writer, and Daniel Fogarty, president of the Fogarty Construction Company, all of Stockford."

The article went on to explain how Demarest, under the pretext of arranging for a state highway to go near property owned by the victims, had persuaded the four to hand him $45,950 in cash to cover the "costs of the arrangement." Demarest had, of course, put up the rest of the money, $14,050, himself as evidence of "good faith" and then had promptly disappeared, leaving Randolph $20,000 poorer, Wilcox $11,550, Fogarty $9000 and Somers $5400. It was the age-old classic version of the con game, worked, the story suggested, by playing on man's cupidity. The foursome had hoped to reap huge profits from the mythical highway and Demarest had preyed on their desires.

Though the story concentrated on Demarest, showing him off first as a con man and then as something more—a murderer as well—the details reflected obvious discredit on his victims and there was shock and consternation in four Stockford homes that evening.

Carleton Randolph learned of it when he came in at five-thirty from showing a client some property. Dixie met him at the door with a sober face and the paper in her hand. She said to him, "It's come out," and pointed to the article. He seized the paper and devoured the story, his face turning purple. "Who did it? That's what I want to know. Who told!?"

"A reporter called up this morning. He asked me if you'd

given George twenty thousand dollars. He told me it was you who gave him the story and he was just checking back on figures."

Randolph gaped at her. "I? The liar. I never said a word. Did you tell him?"

Dixie smiled faintly. "Now, Sugar, you know me better than that. I told him I didn't have any idea what he was talking about."

"Someone told him and I want to know who. Believe me, George isn't the only one, I could commit a few murders myself."

"Is it all that terrible, dear? I mean, maybe the story does let on, without saying so, that you wanted to pay to get the highway to go by our land, but is that so terrible? How many people in this world wouldn't, if they had a chance?"

"It's worse than that. It's not that the story makes me look naughty. That's bad enough. But it makes me look stupid! To have been taken in like that!"

"But you mustn't blame yourself. It was all so perfectly logical."

"Of course it was perfectly logical. At least it sounded so at the time. That's how those con artists always operate. They've got a perfectly logical story to tell. It's only after you've been bilked that you see how stupid you were. And we *were* stupid! That whole damned story he told. Those people he brought in. The Big Boy up in Hartford who was going to arrange the whole thing! How the hell I was ever fool enough to be sucked into that, I don't know. It stinks!" He turned to her. "It's because he had property there too, because he had a reputation in town. He sold insurance, for Christ's sake. You don't expect an insurance agent . . . You don't figure . . . And he had the land before I did. It didn't look like a con game at all. He had the land, the house. He looked well fixed. How the hell was I to know he was broke?"

Dixie was soothing. "Baby, baby," she said. "Your heart. You're getting all red in the face. You didn't get excited like this when it happened. Don't get so upset now."

"I didn't then because I still didn't really believe it. I thought he'd just been tempted. I thought he only stole from us. I didn't know he set out deliberately to cheat us. But you read the story, you can see it. And now everybody in town knows it. I'm going to be a laughing stock. Carleton Randolph, shrewd real estate operator, gets taken for twenty grand. And in a real estate deal to boot. His own field! And I'm the *biggest* fool. I paid out almost half of the total. And I do it to try to bribe government officials. Oh, Jesus." He strode to the phone.

"Now who? Fogarty again? I'll bet he's the son of a bitch," Dixie said as he dialed, "Baby, your blood pressure."

Fogarty had already seen the paper and he didn't take kindly to Randolph's opening remarks. "What're you trying to accuse me of," he shouted back into the phone. "You think I like that kind of crap appearing in the papers?"

Randolph said, "Are you trying to deny you told that story to the reporters?"

"Yes I'm denying it. But what I'm telling you is you've got a big nerve accusing me. Why don't you accuse some of your pals?"

"All right, if it wasn't you, it was your stupid wife."

"Don't you call my wife stupid or I'll put a handful of knuckles through your teeth."

"Did you ask her if she told?"

"Why don't you ask your wife? Whattaya think, Dixie's so pure and innocent?"

"She didn't tell. When the reporters came around, she told them nothing."

"Well when they came around I didn't tell them nothing either. And neither did Mary."

"Oh, the reporters talked to you? Did they say who *did* tell?"

"Yes, if you want to know. They said it was Warren. They said he spilled the beans."

"They said it was Warren?"

"That's what they told me, so take back what you said."

"That depends on whether you told them any more."

"I didn't tell them a thing. And Mary's right here and she's got a message for you. She says, 'Shove it up your ass.'" Fogarty slammed down the phone.

Randolph didn't get to call Stan Somers. Somers called him while he was trying to reach Wilcox. "Did you see the papers?" Stan said. "That does it."

"Does what?"

"That ends it with Jerry."

"You mean she told?"

"I don't know. She's in Pittsfield, shopping, But I'm telling you I'm walking out. But you're not to tell her."

"Well, I don't get it. What do you mean?"

"Just what I said. I'm clearing out."

Randolph, worried at the prospect of having a permanent guest again, said, "Well wait a minute. If she didn't do it—"

"I didn't say she didn't do it. She probably did for all I know."

"But if she didn't—"

"It doesn't matter. You talked me into going back to her to keep this thing quiet. Well it's not quiet any longer and it doesn't matter who let it out. Frankly, I'm just as glad because now I've got an excuse to leave her for good."

"But why, Stan? I mean, you're back with her."

"You know why."

"But she's not seeing Warren any more."

"I don't give a damn whether she sees him or whether she doesn't—or whether she sees anybody. It's too late. I told you that. I told you we're through. I just went back to make it look good."

"Yes, but—well, I thought—I thought maybe Deirdre's being dead—I mean, doesn't that make any difference?"

"No that doesn't make any difference. The news has broken. In fact, I'm not at all sorry. It's painful and it makes us look like a bunch of slimy fools but that's only a temporary pain. Playing husband to Jerry was an enduring one."

"Maybe you just kind of dropped a hint to the papers so you could move out of Jerrys bed and board and take up lodgings elsewhere."

"Well if you aren't one son of a bitch. Fogarty was the one who gave out the story. A reporter was around trying to pump me. He claimed Fogarty had told him the whole story."

"That son of a bitch."

"You're another."

When Randolph finally reached Wilcox, he was really red-faced and fuming and Dixie was trying in vain to soothe him. As for Wilcox, he was trying to be suave but having trouble. "Yes I saw it," he said. "I was going to call you. The reporter said you did it. He said you blew it all."

"That's a God damned lie," Randolph shouted. "I'm the one who told the rest of you to keep your mouths shut, remember? That reporter was tricking you. He was making you believe he knew the whole story and you fell for it and *gave* him the story."

"I did no such thing."

"That reporter told Dixie you did. He told the others you did too."

"And he told me you did it. It was a trick, just as you said. So maybe you did it or maybe somebody else did. All I know is it wasn't I."

"Maybe it was Moira."

"It wasn't Moira. She wouldn't do a thing like that."

"You don't think she'd like to see you in trouble?"

"No."

"A hell of a psychiatrist you are. It sticks out all over her.

You and your fooling around. You think she's going to like that? Where the hell did you learn your job?"

Wilcox got testy. "Don't you talk about my job. I know my business and that's more than you can say. You, a big real estate man, letting yourself get conned out of twenty thousand dollars on a real estate deal! I wouldn't buy a flowerbed from you."

"Yeah, well if you're so great, why don't you cure that sick wife of yours?"

"My wife isn't sick. She's just as normal as you are."

"You really think so? Then you're sicker than she is. Why don't you cure yourself, if you're such a great doctor? A man your age chasing after every skirt he sees. You ought to be *getting* treatment, not giving it."

"My, my," Wilcox retorted, regaining some composure. "Aren't we aggressive this evening. What fears are you hiding behind all that anger, Carleton? What are you running away from?"

That was the kind of tack Randolph couldn't cope with. He slammed the phone down so hard it made Wilcox wince. The psychiatrist made a face and hung up his own receiver. He went back to the dinner table where Moira, pausing in her eating, said, "My, don't we have a charming telephone personality."

"You were listening."

"How could I help but hear you?"

"I had the door closed. You couldn't hear me from the table. You got up and eavesdropped. That's what you did. In my own house I've got a wife who—"

"A wife who wants to know what women are calling you up. That's who."

"Don't feed me your lies. If there were any women, do you think they'd call me at my home? You're the one who gave that story to the press. That's what the real truth is."

"That's right," she whined. "Blame me for everything. Make me your scapegoat."

"It was you and don't deny it."

"You never get blamed for anything. You always find a way to weasel out of everything. Like the way you're always weaseling out of admitting what you were doing with Deirdre and Jerry."

"'Me and the women. All right, then, if that's the way you want it. And now ask yourself what else do you expect when I'm married to a de-sexed nothing like you?"

"Ah, you admit it! There are women. The truth comes out."

"Yes, there are women. Now are you satisfied?"

"I knew there were women. And when George gave you a black eye for fooling around with his wife, you turned to Stan's wife because Stan wasn't as big and strong as George."

"I was through with Deirdre long before any trouble with George."

"So there *was* trouble with George. He *did* black your eye. I knew it." She sounded almost gleeful. And it was about Deirdre, no matter what you say. He punched you to make you stay away from her."

"It was not. It was because I was through with her and she didn't like it. So she told lies to George."

"Why other women?" Moira's voice broke. "Why?"

"Because I'm married to you."

"You blame me." She started to weep a little.

"Do you think I get any satisfaction from you? Ask yourself who's the frigid one in this family."

"You've always got an answer that leaves you in the clear, free to do whatever you want, free to go with whatever woman comes along."

"Sure, that's right. It's all me. So why don't you get a divorce?"

"Oh, certainly. That's the easy answer. Get a divorce. And then what?"

"Then go find someone more to your liking."

"And that's so easy at my age, isn't it? Throw me out and tell me to go find somebody else, after you've used up all my youth and appeal and left me neurotic and sick and not fit for anybody."

"So stay single. You'd get plenty of alimony. You wouldn't have to worry."

"You'd like that. You'd really like that. I'm getting in your way. I'm starting to complain about the way you carry on. You don't want that. It doesn't do your conscience any good. Up till now you could always pretend I was sick when I accused you of having other women. But not any more. Now you've admitted it. So now you've got another answer. Divorce. Get me out of the way. You don't owe me anything. A little alimony will give you a clear conscience on that. Then you're free and can lead your happy little life. Well it's not going to be like that. You're not throwing me out of your life."

"So don't get a divorce."

"And you're not shutting me out of your life here. I'm someone you're going to have to reckon with, Warren Wilcox. I'm not going to be put aside."

"Stay or go, I don't care. Just keep out of my way, that's all."

20

The inquest Thursday afternoon drew thirty spectators, newsmen Lawrence and Harrington, County Coroner Clement Avery, and the witnesses. It lasted half an hour, or only long enough for MacFarlane to tell the cause of death and for Fellows to reveal how the police had become involved in the case, the clue of the used shovel, the clue of the glasses case and the footprint. Clement Avery was not the Grand Jury and the inquest itself had no authority, but the political position of county coroner gave few opportunities for the kind of publicity murders produced and he announced his verdict as if the Voice of Doom were speaking. "The finding of this inquest," he intoned sonorously, "is that the deceased, Deirdre Demarest, was shot and killed by her husband, George Demarest, aided and abetted by a woman unknown."

Harrington, sitting beside Fellows, muttered "Crap," and stood up as Avery left.

Fellows smiled. "Why did you bother coming?"

"Because you never know. Though I ought to by now. You're not going to get a good story from the officials. If you want anything good, you've got to dig it out yourself."

"Which reminds me," Fellows said, moving to the door and the stairs, "that was some story you dug up for last night's paper."

"Yeah. No thanks to you. I'll bet none of it was news to you either."

"Who'd you get it from?"

"The lot of them. Randolph gave it away to begin with, of course. Then it was just a question of checking with the town clerk on Monday to find out who owned the rest of the property out there, getting on the phone and calling them."

"And you got them to confess all?"

"No problem. Just the old cop trick—telling each one I'd been given the story by one of the others. Then I sat back and listened while they tarred each other black trying to whitewash themselves." He snorted. "Some bunch of clucks. No wonder Demarest took them for a ride."

"Very enterprising, Mr. Harrington."

"No thanks to you, Fellows. You could have told me who owned that property on Friday and saved me three days. But that's what I say. You never get any stories from the officials."

"Oh, once in a while we try to cooperate. I've got a story for you right now, in fact. If you're interested."

"Yeah? Like what? Like you can't find out where Demarest got his rifle?"

"It's a little better than that. There's been another sighting."

"Demarest has been seen again? What'd he do this time? Rob a drugstore?"

"Not quite. A man resembling Demarest, accompanied by a tall bleached blonde, stayed last night in a motel outside of Pittsburgh. They registered as Mr. and Mrs. Douglas Cotter and were driving a Volkswagen squareback with Connecticut plates. The motel owner didn't get the license."

Harrington got out his notebook and wrote that down as they approached headquarters through the basement corridor. "And what are you doing about it?"

"Checking with Motor Vehicles."

Three other reporters were gathered in headquarters for any late news and Fellows passed that on to them as well. That was all he had to offer that meant anything.

They went out but a new visitor came in. His name, he said, was Session Arnold and he was a lawyer hired by George Demarest's family in Shoreham. He'd just been to the inquest and he'd like to talk.

Fellows brought him into his office, sat him at the table, and took his chair at the cluttered, rolltop desk. "All right, Mr. Arnold."

Arnold, a dark, chunky man with sharp eyes and an aggressive manner, laid a doubled fist on the table and leaned forward. "The family has hired me," he said, "to represent George Demarest's interests."

Fellows nodded. "And you'd like something from me?"

Arnold said in a hurt tone, "Frankly, Chief, I'm surprised. I'm surprised at you."

"Oh?"

"I'm surprised at that inquest."

"Oh?"

"To accuse a man of murder is the most serious charge that can be brought against an individual."

"Yes, it is."

"I would have expected, in view of the seriousness of the charge, a little more responsibility on the part of the county coroner and of yourself."

"You would?"

"Don't you realize that Demarest is being branded a murderer on the most flimsy circumstantial evidence imaginable? A shovel in his garage. What does that prove? Do you have a bill of sale proving he bought that shovel? Anybody could have put that shovel in his garage. A glasses case. Anybody could have left his glasses case at the scene of the grave. Yet on those two points, and those alone, you brand George Demarest a murderer."

"Correction. That was the county coroner."

"This afternoon it was the county coroner, and frankly I have my reservations regarding the competence of the county coroner. But before this afternoon it's been you who's branded George a murderer."

"Correction again. We've been looking for George to question him in regard to the death of his wife."

"That's just words. Everybody knows you think he did it. And because you think he did it, the public thinks he did it. Now I ask you, is that the American way? Is that your concept of a man being innocent till proven guilty?"

Fellows smiled. "Now, Mr. Arnold, what would you have me do? Not look for George?"

"What I think you should do, Mr. Fellows, is make it clear to the press and public that you've got nothing on this man. I think you should spell it out that the shovel and the glasses case aren't evidence at all, that anyone could have put those items where they were found and that there's every reason to believe someone else left them there to throw suspicion on George."

"Thank you," Fellows said. "And just who is this someone who so conveniently has George's glasses case?"

"Who says it's George's glasses case? Anyone can have any initials he wants stamped on a glasses case."

"That may be true but the case was identified by the optometrist as belonging to George and the glasses they contained were ground to his prescription."

"They could have been stolen from George then. You cannot make me believe for one minute that any man murdering his wife would leave his glasses case at the burial site for everyone to see. And what about a gun? Is there one shred of evidence in your possession that George ever owned a gun, that he ever even shot a gun? You don't have one single concrete piece of evidence against George Demarest and you know it. In court, let me tell you, I'd get an acquittal so fast you'd look like a prize idiot. What about George's nature— the kind of man he was? I've been talking to a lot of people

96

in Shoreham and down here since Monday and I can tell you George just plain isn't the type to kill anybody. I've talked to his family, to friends he grew up with and they'll all testify that George was an industrious, sober, level-headed gentleman."

"Who happened to fool around with women," Fellows said mildly.

"One woman. And he married that woman. Nobody can point a finger at any other woman that George ever had anything to do with except Deirdre Fredericks. And he honorably divorced his wife and married her. She was no passing fancy, she was the great love of his life."

"And he was the great love of hers?"

"Oh, I know there's a lot of talk about her. And I don't deny some of it may be true. But that doesn't mean he didn't love her. He married her, didn't he? Married her knowing what she was—that she got pregnant in high school, for example."

"Did he know this?"

"I'm sure it's not the kind of secret she could have kept from him. And I'll tell you something else. I talked to Mrs. Wilcox this morning. And she told me frankly that her husband was making a play for Deirdre and that George gave him a black eye for it. She told me her husband admitted it to her just last night. Now I don't know how far the playing went, but George knew about it and he beat up Warren Wilcox. That is not the attitude of a man who wants to kill his wife. I'll get psychiatrists up on the witness stand—if you every try to bring George to trial—who will swear under oath that a man who beats up another man for fooling with his wife is not about to murder that wife. If he had that kind of a plan in mind, he would ignore the man—pretend he didn't know about it. He wouldn't even care.

"So you see, Chief, you and the press and the county coroner are giving my client a dirty and unfair deal. You're convicting him before he's ever brought to trial."

Fellows scratched his cheek. "Now that's very interesting about Mrs. Wilcox's story," he said. "That her husband and George had a fight is a nice piece of news in that it indicates George did know what was going on. I wasn't sure about that. But what is of particular interest is that Mrs. Wilcox would tell you this."

"I'm good at getting information."

"That may not be all of it." The chief tilted his chair back. "As for the points you make protesting George's innocence, I'm perfectly willing to hear his story. I'd be delighted to hear his story, in fact. Inasmuch as he's a suspect in the case, I find it hard to understand why, if he's innocent, he doesn't come forward and tell us his story. Maybe he could tell us, for example, who stole his glasses. And why this man, who wants to frame him, buried Mrs. Demarest and left the glasses in a spot where they might not have been found for years—until Mrs. Demarest was nothing but a skeleton and the glasses case rotted away. I'd sure like to hear what he has to say about that. And, of course, the woman's footprint. Maybe it was a woman who framed him. And then, of course, since he's a sober and industrious insurance agent, I'd enjoy hearing him tell what he did with that sixty thousand dollars. And, of course, I'd like to know why he went away. I'm sure he's got a good answer to that one too."

"Just because a man steals money doesn't make him a murderer."

"It doesn't make him a sober, solid citizen either. As for the gun, I admit we don't have any evidence as to his purchasing such a weapon and we have checked all the shops where he could have bought one in the area. But then, we wouldn't expect him or anyone else planning a murder to purchase the weapon where it can be readily traced back to him."

"And that's just what I've been saying. You don't have anything but some flimsy circumstantial evidence. You claim he's with a woman, for example, but you can't show me where he knows any woman. You don't have any proof."

"Not yet we don't. Well, Mr. Arnold, my business is to ask him some questions about his actions. If he's innocent of any crime, that's fine with me. But the fastest way to clear that matter up would be for him to talk to us. I hope, if you have any contact with him, you'll persuade him to do just that?"

"I will assure you, Chief, that I will do what I think is in the best interests of my client."

"I hope you will consider the best interests of justice as well."

Arnold got up. "You talk about justice," he sneered. "All the time you brand him a killer."

"When did I do that?"

"Well, you let the press imply that's what he is and you don't raise a finger to stop it."

"Newspaper work doesn't happen to be my province. But any oversights on my part I'm sure you can correct with statements of your own."

"And don't think I won't make plenty of them."

Arnold walked out as Wilks came in. Fellows told him of

the visit. "Of course he's right," he said. "The evidence is circumstantial."

"It usually is in murder cases—at least where the murder is premeditated."

"He complains we don't have a girl-friend for George. But, of course, that can change any moment."

"It hasn't changed yet." Wilks sat down and stretched out his legs wearily. "Ed and I have finished checking out sixty-nine of those hundred and twenty-one women on Demarest's sucker list. They're all present and accounted for."

21

On Friday, September 23, Missouri State Police captured a man named Edwin Porter after a long chase and a running gunfight. Search of his car revealed an armory of guns and eight thousand dollars. Leslie Duncan, a Tulsa bank teller, identified him as the man who had robbed the bank on Monday the nineteenth. The gunman bore only a superficial resemblance to George Demarest.

That, and a blast against press treatment of Demarest, issued by Session Arnold, was the only news in the case over the weekend. In fact, that was all there was in the case. There were no further sightings. No missing women were uncovered. No women were linked in any way with the fugitive. Attempts to trace the purchase of the rifle ended in failure and even the motel sighting in Pittsburgh didn't pan out. Motor Vehicles had a record of a Douglas Cotter owning a Volkswagen squareback.

By Monday, September 25, the only Stockford police activity still connected with the murder was the wrap-up of the investigation of the hundred and twenty-one women Demarest had seen about insurance since his marriage to Deirdre. That was so unpromising that, though eighteen names remained for checking on Tuesday, Wilks had already given up on it when he returned from the chore Monday afternoon. "There's nothing," he said glumly to Fellows and threw himself into a chair. "Ed hasn't called in, of course?"

"No, but he's due."

"He's got nothing. Tomorrow we'll finish and there'll still be nothing. If some dame had skipped, we'd have heard about it by now."

"I suppose so." Fellows finished making an entry in the blotter and laid down the pen. "And I'd have bet," he said, half to himself, "that she *had* to be somebody he met on his calls. Where else could he have met her without some friend or some acquaintance knowing about it?"

"Maybe she lives on Staten Island," Wilks said sourly. "Say, I just thought of something. Could that car on Staten Island be a blind?"

"I suppose it could," Fellows said. "A blind for what?"

"Check me on this. We're not supposed to know George murdered his wife and ran off with another woman, right? It's supposed to look as though he and Deirdre fled with the money. Why do we believe they've fled with the money? Because he and Deirdre are missing and the car is missing.

"Now they've got to stay missing. Deirdre's buried so she'll be missing permanently. How does he keep the car missing? By abandoning it in a different state without license plates. If it's found, the police might check its serial number through Motor Vehicles in New York—if they wanted to take the trouble. What they wouldn't try doing would be to check with other motor vehicle departments in other states. They'll only check stolen car lists and things."

Fellows said, "And the idea is that he doesn't flee?"

"Look, he kills his wife. There's another woman. She doesn't want to disappear with him. Maybe she can't afford to. What if Deirdre's body is found? What if we can connect her and George? If she and George disappear together, it's not going to look good."

Fellows' eyebrows lifted. "And," he said, with the trace of excitement in his voice, "the reason no woman is missing is because she didn't go away. And neither did George. He dumped the car and came back."

"Right. And instead of being out in Missouri or Pittsburgh, he's right around Stockford, hiding out."

"And seeing this woman."

"Just as quietly as he saw her beforehand. Nobody suspects a thing!"

Detective Sergeant Edward Lewis, who had come in with coffee, said, "And where would he stay? We can check out motels in the area."

"He'd rent a room or a flat or a house somewhere," Wilks said.

Fellows rubbed his chin. "Not too fast. He's being hunted for murder. His picture's been in the papers. He'd be running the risk of some landlord reporting it."

Wilks said, "Maybe he pitched a tent on his property."

Fellows smiled. "That really would be love, wouldn't it? No, we'd better check out all the motels, hotels, inns, flats and the rest everywhere around. But we'd better try to think of where else he might go. Somebody's summer cottage, or somebody's extra house. Someplace where no record would be kept."

"Real estate." Wilks' eyes opened a little. "Say, I just wonder. Do you suppose he and Dixie Randolph—? I'll bet her shoes would fit our footprint."

"So would Mary Fogarty's, Moira Wilcox's and Jerry Somers'. And they don't have alibis. Dixie Randolph does. She's the only one who was with her husband the rest of that evening after the pay-off."

"If the murder took place that night, like we've been thinking. But maybe it didn't."

"If it didn't, you've got to explain how Deirdre came to be wearing the same party frock." Fellows shrugged. "But there's no use speculating until we check some of this stuff out. And one thing we should do is find out what other properties those women own. Or their husbands."

Lewis said, "You think one of them would be the woman?"

Fellows sipped some coffee. Then he rubbed his face. "I don't know why, Ed, but I have a feeling. Five couples thrown together in a common enterprise. They get along fine, or seem to, until things start going wrong. Then all hell breaks loose. I don't know. Maybe the woman is one of those in Demarest's files but I have a hunch the key lies in that group. Maybe it's the way those people rub against each other, but I've got a feeling."

The door opened and Robert Armbruster came in. The chief got up. "Yes, Mr. Armbruster. What'd you find out? How much did Demarest steal?"

"Believe me. What a relief! He didn't steal from us after all. Only from those friends of his."

"He didn't take a thing?"

"Not a penny. Checks are there—from his customers. Made out to him. Uncashed. It's all there. What a relief," he said and hurried out.

Fellows said, "Well I'll be damned."

22

Jerry Somers lighted a cigarette while holding the phone at her ear. The intermittent buzzes were interrupted and Dixie Randolph said hello at the other end. Jerry took a quick drag, said, "Dixie? Jerry. Is Stan there?"

"Why no," Dixie said innocently. "Isn't he with you?"

"If he was I wouldn't be asking. He went to New York Thursday and he hasn't shown up here yet. I just looked in his closet and it appears he took more than an overnight bag when he drove out of here. Most of his clothes are gone. And seeing as how he parked in with you before—"

"No, he's not here."

"I'm going to report him missing!"

"Report him?"

"Report him. To the police."

"Listen, Jerry. Wait. Hold on a minute."

There was a delayed pause and then Carl Randolph came on the line. "Now what's this, Jerry? I don't understand all this."

"I don't understand it either. All I know is Stan went to New York Thursday. At least that's where he was supposed to be going and I presume he did because I watched the show last night and the show went on and his name was on the credits and all the rest. Now I know he sometimes stays over till Saturday when there's a lot of work to be done and I know that once they had so much trouble they couldn't tape it until Sunday morning and he didn't get home till Sunday afternoon. But that show went on the air last night and he should have been home long before this and I want to know why he isn't."

"I don't know why," Randolph said and tried to mean it. "Maybe he's still in New York. You know, conferences or something."

"Without letting me know?"

"Well, you know men."

"I know men all right. He should be home and if he's not with you, then nobody knows where he is and I'm going to call the police."

"Now, Jerry, you can't do that."

"Who says I can't?"

"Think of the publicity. Think of the mess."

"That's exactly what I'm thinking of. So either he phones

me right away and explains what this is all about or I call up the police. You can pass that word around."

"Pass it around? To who?"

"To Stan. You're his cousin. He goes to you. And if he's not with you, you know where he is. So if he doesn't want his name all over the papers, he'd better get in touch with me in one hour."

"Jerry, wait a minute. I don't know where Stan is. I honestly don't."

"Then you'd better start finding out."

"Look, I wouldn't know where he'd be. He's probably staying in New York."

"Why? That's what I want to know. Why?"

"Well, maybe he's—ah—leaving you. You know, he did that before."

"He did that and he came back, crawling. He wouldn't run off again. He's got no reason."

"Well, I don't know, then. There must be some explanation."

"There damned well must be and if he isn't leaving me, then he really *is* missing. He's had an accident or something. And that's why I'm going to notify the police."

Carl had no choice. "All right, look," he said and braced himself. "Let me tell you something. He did leave you. I don't know where he went but he told me that's what he was going to do. I didn't want him to, believe me. In fact, we had an awful row about it."

Jerry, stunned, stared at the phone for a moment. "But why?" she said, smashing out her cigarette. "What was the reason?"

"Well—he thought. You know the publicity last Wednesday? All about us? Well, he thought you blabbed to the papers."

"He thought I *what*? He thought I—? That's a filthy lie. Moira Wilcox and the Fogartys are the ones who blabbed. A reporter told me so."

"Maybe he had it mixed up. He certainly thought—"

"I've got to get in touch with him. There's been a mistake. He's not going to leave me because he thought I did a thing like that. How could he?" She stopped. "He didn't accuse me of anything. He just walked out. Somebody must have lied to him. Somebody must have spread a story—"

"Maybe one of the reporters."

"Why would they do that? It was Moira and the Fogartys so why would the reporters say it was me? No. Someone *wanted* him to leave me. Somebody told him that deliberately. Somebody in this group wants to break up my marriage. By

103

God, I'm going to find Stan and then I'm going to find out who."

Randolph bit his lip and said, "Now take it easy, Jerry—"

"Take it easy? You can sit there in your big fat house, happy as a clam, and tell me to take it easy when someone—"

"Jerry, nobody's trying to break up your marriage."

"Was it you, Carl? He listens to you. He believes you. You're the only one in the group he does believe."

"No. I'm the one who got him to go back to you."

Jerry stopped for a moment. Then she said, "Say that again."

"Well, I mean—"

"I heard you. You said you got him to come back to me. You'd better explain that and explain it fast."

"I only meant I pointed out how lucky he was to have you, that he was the pot calling the kettle black, that he ought to reconsider. And he did."

"And that made him change his mind?"

"Yes. He saw the error of his ways."

"What else did you say?"

"What do you mean, what else?"

"I mean that's exactly what *I* told him. That didn't even slow him down in his packing."

"Well, you said I have influence."

"And you 'got' him to come back to me. That's more than influence, my fat friend. That's pressure. So he's supposed to leave me a second time because he thinks I blabbed to the press? Without even accusing me, without even a goodbye, he takes off. He didn't come back to me to *keep* me from blabbing, did he? You didn't tell him to go back to Jerry to shut her up, did you?"

"Now listen, Jerry, he wanted to go back to you."

"Yes, that's what I thought. That's what I wanted to think. And I was just blind enough and dumb enough to believe it. But not any more. You didn't want the story to come out and I was threatening to spill it and so little Stanley comes trotting back with apologies, hoping against hope I'll tell him to go to hell. But I don't and he makes like it's almost the way it was before and then the story breaks anyway. Jerry kept quiet but Moira and the Fogartys talked. So Stanley doesn't have to stay any more. That's the way it was, wasn't it?"

"No honestly, he wanted to go back. He realized he'd made a mistake."

"Then why did he go away again?"

"I—well, I—I just can't imagine. But he was saying to me

how much he wanted to go back to you but he had too much pride. Honest he was."

"Pride, my ass! He crawled. He crawled to keep me quiet. And you put him up to it. There's only one kind of slimy creature worse than you. And that's him. And just let me tell you this, fat man. If you think I was going to blow the whistle before, you wait and see what happens now."

23

At half-past nine that Monday night, Chief Fellows rang the door of Sid Wilks' house. Marge answered and said, "Hello, Fred. He's down in the cellar." Unannounced calls by the chief of police meant one thing to Marge. He had questions and answers and he wanted to try them out on her husband.

Sid Wilks' cellar looked like a railroad yard in miniature. Model trains were his hobby and he built engines and cars and laid track and most of what money was left over after the rent, groceries and modest living expenses were taken care of went into the purchase of HO equipment.

Fellows ducked under the hanging cellar light and moved in where the fluorescent tubes illuminated the main track area. "That one giving you trouble?"

"Some. But I have an idea you're going to give me more. It's bad enough I don't get any days off, now I have to work nights."

"Wouldn't life be easy if there weren't any criminals?"

"It wouldn't be real." Wilks shut down the transformer and spit tobacco into a pail. "I have an idea," he said, "that you didn't come here to tell me who the woman in George's life is. You've got something else on your mind."

"That's right. A big fat question."

"Which is?"

"Why didn't George Demarest take the insurance payments with him too? Why only the sixty thousand dollars? He scrapes and scrounges to raise every cent of cash he can get for himself, puts himself in hock to the eyeballs to ante up fourteen thousand and fifty dollars, but he doesn't take a cent from the insurance company and it's there for the grabbing. Why?"

"All right, I don't know. What's going on inside that skull of yours?"

"I'll tell you what's going on. When I heard that, it made no sense at all. And then I began to realize none of the rest of it makes any sense either. All the pieces of the puzzle we've been working on, all the ideas we've had, all the angles, they just don't fit together into any kind of coherent picture. Look, we know the guy's broke. He's banking on the highway deal but that falls through. So we have him fleecing his greedy friends with a con job any pro would be proud of. But he's an insurance agent. That's about as far removed from a con man as you can get. Yet this inexperienced guy trims four friends out of forty-six thousand dollars. And that kind of money, for con artists, is very big time. Any con man would drool.

"And how does he get this money? Not in an insurance swindle, mind you, Not in the field he knows. He gets it with a real estate deal!

"And who does he work the deal on? Only a shrewd contractor and the top real estate agent in this whole area!

"Now I ask you, Sid. When you wake up and stand off and take a good look at that setup, is that believable? Grant that it could be done, would he ever in his life be fool enough to try it? Who would dare?"

Wilks, staring at the floor, shook his head. "Doesn't seem likely."

"So let's say, instead, that Demarest wasn't trying to con anybody. The highway bribery deal is real and it's not a swindle he's worked, it's a double-cross. He kills his wife, cheats his friends, gives up his business, property, and reputation. O.K.? This is all for love of a woman, right? He'll do anything for this woman. Except steal money from the Northeastern Insurance Company.

"All right, let's consider George and this woman he's so much in love with, this mysterious woman who leaves no fingerprints, no lipstick traces, no smell of perfume behind her, no gossip even. Nothing but a footprint. All we know about her is that she's three to five inches taller than Deirdre. That's not much, but that's quite an important point.

"We've had them fleeing. But abandoning the car on Staten Island gives that a funny look. So now we have your new theory. The whole flight is a ruse. Let's examine it from that angle now. Let's try to reconstruct.

"It's the night of August twenty-fourth. George Demarest receives all this money from his buddies. The wives are all there. They're all together. They count out the money and they all go home. Then, sometime thereafter, George shoots Deirdre and some woman comes around. He and the woman drive Deirdre's body into the woods in his station wagon to a pre-dug grave. They return. He switches cars and takes off in the Thunderbird. This is to make us think he's fled, right?"

"That was the general thought."

"Then he holes up somewhere and continues to meet this woman on the sly."

Wilks said, "I admit I've heard better stories."

"Let's go on. George wants it to appear that he and Deirdre have gone away. To foster that idea, he's taken suitcases full of their clothes. All summer clothes. No winter clothes. That's to make us think they've gone to warmer climes. That'll throw us off the track, right?"

"Right."

"So here's the question. What did he do with those clothes?"

"He's probably wearing them."

"His, but not hers. What would he do with hers? They won't fit his lady-friend. She's three to five inches taller, remember? And as for him, if he's going to hang out in *this* area, assuming another identity and disguise, why would he only take summer clothes? Winter's coming."

Wilks rubbed his chin. "I guess I don't know."

"There were no suitcases left in his house. And judging from the empty drawers and hangers, enough clothes were taken away to fill at least four suitcases. We've got to figure him with four suitcases. Now he certainly wouldn't take them to Staten Island and lug them back with him on the ferry. He'd have to drop them off at his hideout. Or his girl-friend would have to take them in her car. Either way, this presupposes a hideout. But this has flaws in it, because while he might want his own clothes, Deirdre's suitcases would be an albatross around his neck. If he's going to pretend he isn't George Demarest, which is what he's got to do whether he's hiding out here or fleeing somewhere else, he's going to want those suitcases to disappear just as completely as his wife does. So what would he do with them?"

"There are lots of possibilities. He could hide them in all kinds of places we'd never find."

"Sure he could, but why would he overlook the most logical place of all? Why didn't he throw them in the grave with his wife?"

Wilks pondered that one. "I don't know," he finally said. "There's probably a good reason. If we knew what was going on in George's mind—"

"Think of the dimensions of that grave. Eight and a half by four. He didn't have to dig it that big. Six by three would have been ample."

"Then he was going to put the suitcases in with her and something changed his mind?"

"Such as what?"

"I'm not George. I wouldn't be able to guess."

"And that's what I'm talking about. Nothing in this case comes out right. We find clues and the clues tell us stories. But the stories don't fit together. Let's go back to that outsized grave again. Deirdre was two to two and a half feet below ground. That's plenty deep enough to have thrown the suitcases in on top of her. You still don't need to dig an eight and a half by four foot hole."

"True. So we figured he dug it when she wasn't around and wanted to make sure there was plenty of room."

"That's one answer. But there's another. The deeper you're going to dig a hole, the bigger that hole's going to be."

"You think he might have buried the suitcases *under* the body?"

"He might."

"But we did dig under the body."

"Three or four inches. Just to check. Maybe we should have dug farther."

Wilks eyed the chief. "If you want to dig farther, you're not looking for suitcases."

"Oh, but I am."

"Not *just* suitcases. Because you know as well as I do that if he was burying suitcases with a body, he wouldn't put the suitcases under the body. He'd put them all the same depth or the body under the suitcases."

"That's right, but I'm damned curious about that grave now. I want to see what'll happen if, tomorrow morning, I take Harris out there and make him dig down another four feet."

24

Patrolman Edwin C. Harris didn't have to dig down four more feet. He hit the first suitcase two feet deeper. It was a woman's overnight bag, crammed with feminine apparel. Below that were two more suitcases, a woman's and a man's. Then there were loose clothes, dresses and suits still on hangers, and underneath them, at the bottom of the pit, six feet down, a man's body.

Though the digging had started with only Fellows, Wilks and Harris on hand, the exhuming of the body took place before a much larger audience. MacFarlane had to be there to give the order to move the body. Hank Lemmon and his camera were necessary to the occasion, and so were additional policemen. Fellows had summoned two supernumeraries, Armand Sokoloff and his own son, Larry, to keep things under control.

Also present was Jerry Somers, who had once been married to Demarest, Carl and Dixie Randolph, and eight press people.

As for the body itself, final uncovering was done under MacFarlane's direction, dirt being carefully scraped away so as not to damage the remains. The body was clad in brown loafers, green wool socks, tan gabardine pants, white shirt open at the throat with no tie or jacket. The front of the shirt was stained with blood and bore two small holes similar to the twenty-two hole in Deirdre's dress.

When Lemmon had shot his pictures, and when MarFarlane had given permission to remove the remains, Fellows went over to Jerry Somers. "Do you remember how Mr. Demarest was dressed that last night?"

She pictured it in her mind's eye. "Brown sports jacket. Green tie, Tan gabardine slacks, loafers."

"Socks?"

"I don't remember."

The chief went to the Randolphs and repeated the question. Carl could only remember a brown jacket. Dixie did better. She confirmed Jerry's report and added green socks.

"We think it's Demarest," Fellows told Randolph, "He's been underground for a month and isn't very pretty to look at. I'd rather not force Mrs. Somers to look at him if you think you could make an identification."

Randolph went forward with the chief to the edge, looked once and looked away, looked again for a longer time and said, "I think that's George all right."

"Thank you." Fellows turned him loose and went to Mrs. Somers again. "Mr. Randolph believes it's Mr. Demarest. I don't think it's necessary for you to verify it unless you want to."

"No thank you." She mashed the latest cigarette out under her foot. "That means somebody killed both of them?"

"It looks that way. Anything you want to tell us?"

"I'll tell you this much. There isn't a man in that group who couldn't have done it."

"You mean they all had opportunity?"

"I mean who isn't psychologically capable."

"Your husband included?"

"My husband included."

Fellows glanced around. "I notice he didn't come with you. Where is he, by the way?"

"I don't know where he is."

"There's been some trouble?"

"There's been plenty of trouble. And don't let him fool you with his nice innocent air. He's a master of deceit. He's a past-master. All of them are. And I mean to include that fat, grinning real estate entrepreneur and that smooth-talking psychiatrist."

"What about the women? Do you think they're capable of murder too?"

"Let's put it this way. I think any one of them would love to see Deirdre dead."

"Including you?"

That stopped her. She gave the chief a cold look. "That's a fool thing to ask."

Fellows said mildly, "I suppose it is. What show does your husband write for? I don't believe I know."

"The Gary Blake Variety Show. You know, the one that's supposed to give Ed Sullivan competition?"

"I know. I didn't know it had writers."

Jerry sneered. "Where do you think Gary's ad libs come from?"

"I guess I don't know much about those things. Who produces the show?"

"Arfon Productions. But if you're after my husband, don't call them, call Al Fever in Crestwood. He helps Stan write it."

"All right, thanks. I guess you can leave now. One thing. The night all this happened—August twenty-fourth. After the pay-off your husband worked at home on a script?"

"That's right. Most of the night, I understand."

"But you can't support that alibi?"

"He's got a workroom set up in the cellar. When he's down there he might as well be on the moon. I presume he went down there to work. What he really did I wouldn't know."

Fellows thanked her and started back. She headed for her car and Randolph detached himself from Dixie to approach the chief. "What was Jerry telling you?" he asked suspiciously.

Fellows looked at him with mock surprise. "Mr. Randolph, I should think you'd know better than to ask a question like that."

"Well, whatever it was, don't believe too much of what she says. She's out to make Stan and Warren and me look bad."

"Why?"

"Stan's left her because she was fooling around with Warren. And Warren's dropped her too. She's very bitter."

"And what's she got against you?"

"I'm Stan's cousin."

"What kind of an answer is that?"

"She thinks I influenced him to leave her. I didn't. I tried to get him to go back to her."

"I see. By the way, the night of the pay-off, when you and Mrs. Randolph left, you went right home? The both of you? What did you do then?"

"Nothing. Let's see. It was about half-past nine. I think we watched something on television. Then we went to bed after the news. That would be around half-past eleven."

Fellows made a note and told Randolph he could leave. He went back to the grave where efforts were being made to raise the body on a stretcher.

Wilks was there watching. He said, "Well, we've turned up everything but the sixty thousand dollars. What's that old line about always look for the obvious motive? Here we've been chasing all kinds of angles and it's been robbery pure and simple all the time."

"Robbery, maybe. Pure and simple, no. If we went astray all over the place, we had some help. We were led."

"Well, you finally saw through it. Now the question is, who wanted sixty thousand dollars?"

"More to the point: Who was willing to kill two people to get it?"

"Someone who knew the Demarests had sixty thousand dollars to begin with."

"And that leaves us with the Randolphs, the Wilcoxes, the Somerses and the Fogartys."

"And someone named Hal and someone called the Big Boy."

"I think we can forget them. It's closer to home."

"They must have known when the pay-off was going to be. They set it up, didn't they?"

"Sure, but if they wanted to take the money, why wouldn't they let George bring it to them as planned? They wouldn't go into unfamiliar territory to do the job. Besides, who else but someone in that group would dig a hole out here? Who else would know they had to commit murder to get the money —because they're so well known to the Demarests no disguise would fool them?"

Wilks rubbed his chin. "And if somebody else had been chosen to deliver the money instead of Demarest, it would be *that* somebody lying down at the bottom of this hole. You know, thinking about that gives me chills."

They moved away as the ambulance attendants started to raise the stretcher and the reporters crowded around. "I figure it's got to be Somers, Wilcox or Fogarty," Wilks muttered as they strolled off out of earshot. "They're the only ones who don't have alibis. And of the three, it'd be most likely Somers. He'd need the dough the most. Next, Fogarty. You can't tell about him."

"Lots of angles, lots of angles," Fellows muttered, frowning. "For instance, Sid, the glasses case was a planted clue. That's pretty evident now. But what about that woman's footprint? Was that a plant or an accident?"

"Meaning," Wilks said slowly, "that it could have been the Randolphs together?"

"Or Warren Wilcox and Jerry Somers together, or Stan and Moira, or the Fogartys together, or one of the men alone. You can slice it almost any way you want."

"Damn it."

"It's going to be one or more of those eight, Sid. I think you'd better set up watches on them. If someone's got sixty thousand dollars around it's not going to fit in safe-deposit boxes. It's going to be hidden somewhere and now that we know Demarest doesn't have the money, whoever does have it isn't going to want it found on him. Whoever it is may try to re-hide it."

"Right. A watch on everybody."

Stan Somers, by the way, has left Jerry. I don't know what the story is, but I think it's worth finding out. Try a guy named Al Fever in Crestwood."

"I'll talk to him. I'm going to talk to all of them again."

25

Wednesday was normally one of Fellows' days off but he was in his office at half-past ten when Wilks returned from another round of legwork. "It's a damned mess," the detective lieutenant complained. "We're all chasing around and we're getting nowhere."

"No leads?" Fellows asked, biting off some chewing tobacco and checking his watch.

"Oh, we've got all kinds of leads." He took out his notebook. "Moira Wilcox wears a size $8\frac{1}{2}$ shoe. Mary Fogarty wears a $7\frac{1}{2}$. Dixie Randolph wears $8\frac{1}{2}$ and Jerry Somers an 8. The measurements of that cast indicate the shoe that made the print was no smaller than $7\frac{1}{2}$ and no bigger than $8\frac{1}{2}$. That means any of the women could have made it. That is, unless it's a red herring and was planted there to make us think a woman is involved.

"We've asked around at the banks and credit companies and such and we've asked the people themselves point blank. Warren Wilcox claims he takes in between sixty and eighty thousand a year. He's got a safe full of stocks and bonds he invests his leftover money in. Fogarty says he pays himself a salary of fifteen thousand a year. The company makes a lot more. His credit's good at any bank. He's borrowed on many occasions, building the company up, and has always made good. Carleton Randolph averages between thirty and thirty-five thousand a year. He showed me his bank books and checking accounts because he was very anxious for me to understand that he didn't need sixty thousand dollars and therefore wouldn't have robbed George and Deirdre. He's got ten thousand in two different banks in savings, he's got forty-five hundred dollars in one checking account and twenty-eight hundred in another.

"Stan Somers is staying with the Fevers right now. I talked to him there. He claims he made eighteen thousand last year and thirteen so far this year. The Gary Drake show's set for another thirteen weeks anyway so he's employed at least till the end of the year. He can't point to any tangible assets other than a couple of thousand in his checking account, but he claims he doesn't owe on anything except the mortgage on his land and his car. He'll probably have to give Jerry some dough, he says, because he's not going back to her. But, he says he never had any pressing need for sixty thousand dollars. His wife says he owes some other money—a five hundred dollar liquor bill and a few things like that, and she claims he's in real financial trouble, but she can't produce any evidence and it sounds like she's trying to get back at him."

"Get back at him by hanging a murder rap on him?"

"That's the picture I get. Sweet kid." Wilks flipped over a couple of pages. "We already know alibis for that night. As for somebody driving that Thunderbird down to Staten Island, it might have been done the next day. Stan Somers went to New York that Thursday noon. That's August twenty-fifth. He goes every Thursday with his material. His custom is to drive his car to the station and leave it there. He'd pick it up Saturday or Sunday, whenever he came home. Of course on

113

that particular morning, he could have left the car at the station and driven the Thunderbird to Staten Island. There's nothing to say he did or he didn't.

"As for Warren Wilcox, Thursday, August twenty-fifth was the morning he took that book of his down to New York. That's another convenient time. He says he went by train but he can't prove he did and we can't prove he didn't. He could have driven the Thunderbird, ditched it and then turned in the manuscript.

"Anyway, that's an interesting piece of timing—him going down to New York the day after the pay-off and the Thunderbird turning up in Staten Island a few days after that."

"Unfortunately," Fellows said, "that doesn't prove a damned thing."

"Unfortunately. As for Fogarty and Randolph, they claim they haven't been near New York between August twenty-fifth and the date the car turned up. And their wives back them up.

"And, of course, we have a watch on all of those people. They know now that it's robbery, but if someone in that bunch has the money lying around, so far he's not making any moves to hide it somewhere else.

"So that's where we stand as of the present moment. Oh yes, when faced with the idea that robbery was the motive, every one of them believed it had to be Hal or the Big Boy. Everyone except Jerry Somers. Her pick was one of the men in the group. Randolph, Fogarty, Wilcox or Somers. She sees them all as equal villains."

"Who's your choice?"

Wilks sighed and scratched his head. "That's where you've got me. I don't have any choice. There isn't any one in the bunch I like for the job. Not one of those four, not Hal, not the Big Boy. I'd pick the good old mysterious stranger if I could, but even that seems to be out. Nobody outside of the group could have known about the money. The lot of them swear they never breathed a word about it and that's one story they tell that I do believe." He made a face. "So I'm stumped, Fred. Right now I'm stumped. Isn't it about time for you to come up with one of your far-out hunches around now? You got any kind of feelings about this?"

Fellows checked his watch again. "I've got something that I hope is going to be better than a hunch. Instead of trying amateur guesswork, I'm going to patronize the pros."

"What are you talking about?"

"We want to know who did it, don't we? And we want to know what was done with the money, right? Well, at eleven o'clock I have an audience—if that's a good word—with Warren Wilcox and I'm going to ask him those very questions. He knows the people involved. He knows the way their minds work. He's got it all over us in that department. Remember how he was the one who suspected Demarest was in financial trouble when everyone else, ourselves included, thought he was well-fixed? He's the pro and we're the amateurs. So I'm going to put the pro to work on this little problem. Who might have needed the money? Who might have been willing to kill for it? And where would that someone have hidden the money?"

"And you think he'll tell you?"

"He fancies himself a very smart man. I think, if it's put to him right, he'll do his damnedest."

Wilks stroked his chin thoughtfully. "Mind if I listen in?"

"I was hoping you'd want to."

26

The girl in Wilcox's outer office smiled prettily at the two policemen. "Doctor is waiting for you," she cooed. "Please go right in."

"Oh, yes. Chief Fellows. And Lieutenant Wilks." Wilcox rose to shake their hands.

"Nice office," Fellows said and sat down on the couch, making room for the detective lieutenant.

"Yes. I, ah, gather this is something important? I canceled a patient to give you this time."

"I appreciate that. It's very important. Won't you sit down and I'll outline the problem."

Wilcox sat slowly and put on his smile. "I'm certainly interested to hear it."

"Simply put, it's like this. We seem to be up a tree on this Demarest thing. We thought you could help us out."

Wilcox looked puzzled. "Help you out in what way?"

"Your experience as a psychiatrist, your knowledge of the people involved. Look at it this way, Doctor. We have two people murdered, right?"

"And sixty thousand dollars stolen."

"Yes, and that money stolen. What we want from you is your estimate of what kind of a person committed these murders and took that money."

Wilcox smiled and sat back, putting his fingertips together. "I would say that it was done by someone who wanted sixty thousand dollars."

"Could you be a little more specific? After all, I want sixty thousand dollars but I don't kill people for it."

"Then let us say this particular person must have wanted it very badly."

"Who, for example? Of the eight people who knew the Demarests had this money?"

"Eight?"

"The Fogartys, the Somerses, the Randolphs, you and your wife."

Wilcox smiled as if to a small boy. "You're forgetting something, Chief. You will recall my theory, back when we all believed George stole the money? I explained it to the lieutenant. It was that George had hired somebody to play the role of Hal and talk about someone named the Big Boy. Now that we learn George was not the perpetrator of the theft but a victim, we can only conclude that Hal and the Big Boy are real live people. They must exist, Chief, and since they would know Demarest had the money, being the ones who told him to pick it up, we have to say there are ten suspects involved."

"Perhaps you didn't know, Doctor, but the grave was dug in advance. The whole thing was engineered at this end, not the Hartford end. Hal and the Big Boy would hardly come down here for the money when George Demarest was going to take it up there. We've discounted both of them in our calculations." Fellows arched an eyebrow. "As an experienced psychiatrist, do you really believe a valid case can be made for them?"

Wilcox pondered a moment and shook his head. "No. You're quite right about that."

"It would have to be one of the eight."

"Yes. Or, perhaps, more than one."

"Now we're starting to move in the right direction. I know it may be difficult asking you to point a finger at people who are your friends, especially since it would only be guesswork, but it's something I think we have to do."

"Well, it is rather—I don't know what to say."

Fellows gestured. "Oh, I don't expect any snap judgments. I just want you to think about it. It's the kind of thing we policemen do all the time. We're faced with a crime and we think to ourselves, 'what kind of a person could have done it?' But in a case like this you can do that better than we. We can speculate all we want about what kind of a person could have killed those two people and where such a person might have hidden the money, but we don't have much to go on compared to you. You're the one who knows them well, you're the one who's had training in this sort of thing. You have insights that we don't have. For instance, one of the things I've been thinking about is, who wanted to see George and Deirdre dead? Now that's just the kind of angle I'd turn to you on."

"Who wanted to see them dead?" Wilcox repeated.

Fellows shrugged. "They're dead, aren't they? Wouldn't you think that fact's important? Wouldn't that indicate somebody *wanted* them dead?"

"No, not really. They're dead because they stood in the way of someone getting sixty thousand dollars."

Fellows said offhandedly, "Well, of course I don't know much about this, but isn't it Freud's belief that there's no such thing as an accident? In other words, if the robber had to kill to rob it was really because he wanted to kill?"

Wilcox smiled faintly. "I know what you mean and that's true in a sense. But I think if you'll examine this case, you'll find that all of your suspects were so well known to the victims that it would be quite impossible for any one of us to take the money without their knowing who was doing the taking. No disguise would fool them. Therefore, if one needed the money, one also needed to kill. There was really no alternative. Now you mention the fact that the grave was pre-dug. The robber quite obviously knew he would have to commit murder to carry off the robbery and was prepared to kill—not George and Deirdre necessarily—but whichever person happened to be chosen to deliver the money. It could have been any of us that the robber was prepared to kill."

"Ah yes," Fellows said. "That's another angle. How were the Demarests picked for the job? Perhaps you can reflect on how that came about."

"It was a natural consequence of George being familiar with the people involved. He brought down that Hal, for instance. I don't think anybody picked George to make the delivery exactly. I think it was naturally expected of him right from the start."

"But if that's the case, then I think we should very definitely consider the angle about who hated them, don't you?"

"No. I thought I just explained. The robber had to kill."

"But kill both of them?"

"It would be imperative, wouldn't it? He'd try for the money that night, wouldn't he?"

"Well, Doctor, to tell the truth, I'm struck a little by that Freud stuff. We've racked our brains trying to figure who'd need that money. By that I mean who'd commit two murders for it. We can't see any of the suspects doing that and what's more, we can't imagine what they think they could do with the money. I mean, where could they hide it? How could they spend it? It makes me begin to wonder if the money was really the motive after all."

Wilcox said, "As a professional in the field of the mind, I don't think there's any question about the money being the motive."

"And that's what we want. A professional opinion." Fellows got up. "If we could just find that money—if you could fathom the mind of the criminal and guess where he'd put it, then we'd be set. It's robbery pure and simple, just as we—and you—have been figuring. But if that doesn't work, then I think we ought to consider the possibility that there's a different motive involved here. That's what I mean about somebody hating George and Deirdre. If you can't figure out anything on the robbery angle, think about that one, will you? I've been trying to, but you can do it much better."

Wilcox rose uneasily. "You put me on something of a spot," he said. "I don't like it much."

"Work on it, huh?"

"I will. I'll let you know."

He saw them to the door and they shook hands.

Downstairs, leaving the building, Wilks said to Fellows, "I don't get that whole ploy. Do you really think he can figure out where the money's hidden?"

And Fellows snorted, "He knows where it's hidden."

27

Wilks did a quick double-take and stopped dead. "Just a minute. Say that again."

"He knows where the money is. He killed them. He took it. The trouble is proving it. That was what that was all about. I'm trying to flush him."

Wilks started walking again slowly. "And you knew this when you went up there?"

"I would've told you, Sid, but I wanted you innocent. I thought it might help persuade the doctor we're not on to him yet—only getting close."

"Getting close?"

"I want him to think that if we don't find the money pretty soon, we're going to start reading the story right. And since he fancies himself so much smarter than us average types, I don't think he's going to want that—even if we can't prove it. At least that's my hope. In which case, he may try to plant the money. He's probably got it hidden somewhere in those woods, but there's little chance anyone but him could ever find it. And even if we could, I'm sure there'd be no way of proving he put it there. So we cross our fingers and see if he takes the bait."

Wilks said, "All right, all right, now cut out the horsing around. What have you been holding out on me?"

"Nothing." Fellows gave him a look of baby innocence. "Not a thing."

"Come on, Fred. You say Wilcox did it. You've got a reason. Why?"

Fellows grinned at him then. "You ever hear the story of the rancher and the poker game?"

"Oh, no. A story at a time like this?"

Fellows took his arm and led him into a diner. "Come on and we'll have a cup of coffee and I'll tell you all about it. It's a very good story."

"The one about Wilcox?"

"The one about the rancher and the poker game." They sat down and ordered and the chief said, "Once there was this rancher out West, see? Well he'd only get into town about once a month and his idea of celebrating and living it up was to play poker. He was crazy about poker. So there was this one time he comes into town and he meets up with some guys who're just getting up a game on the second floor of the old saloon. Four men. All with black mustaches and shifty eyes. So they play for a bit and he's winning a little and losing a little and then, all of a sudden, he gets a big hand. He's got four sevens. So he bets big and everybody else drops out but one guy, who raises. That goes on for a bit until it takes nearly all the money the rancher has in his kick to call. Then he lays down his four sevens and the other guy lays down four eights.

"The rancher's got almost nothing left but he plays a little longer and then he gets an even bigger hand. Four tens. This time he bets a thousand head of cattle and this same other guy matches him. The rancher lays down his four tens and, to his dismay, the other guy lays down four jacks.

"Well, the rancher decides to play a little longer and suddenly he gets a hand containing four kings. This time he bets his remaining cattle and the deed to the ranch. Then he lays down his four kings but, lo and behold, the other guy lays down four aces. And that, of course, is the end of the story." ﹒

"And the moral is the rancher didn't know when he was being taken?"

"Worse than that, Sid. He never learned anything. He kept on falling into the same trap."

"And as a result, Warren Wilcox is a murderer? You'll have to make the connection a little plainer."

"All right, look. First we learn that Deirdre and George Demarest and sixty thousand dollars are missing. So we come to the very obvious conclusion that George and Deirdre have run off with the money. Right? What other conclusion could we come to?

"But then, all of a sudden, it turns out that that conclusion is wrong because we discover Deirdre Demarest has been killed instead. Not only has she been killed, but George's glasses case and a woman's footprint are found by the body. So now we reach the obvious conclusion that what really happened was that George and some other woman killed Deirdre and took the sixty thousand dollars.

"And then it turns out that that conclusion is also wrong because we discover that George has been killed too. So then we reach the new and obvious conclusion that someone had killed them both in order to steal the sixty thousand dollars they had. As with the first two conclusions, what else would we think?

"Well, unlike that old rancher, the third time around ·is where I stopped. If the first two obvious conclusions were wrong, why should I believe the third one would be right? Remember, it's not as if we'd made natural mistakes. We were deliberately conned into those false conclusions. The evidence had been rigged to make us draw those conclusions. Well then, in that case. wasn't it likely that the evidence had been rigged for us to draw this new conclusion and we were being conned a third time?"

Wilks rubbed his chin. "I don't know. Seems to me it would be just as likely that we'd finally got to the bottom of the matter."

"That's a possibility, of course, and when we found George's body, I admit my suspect list was going to be made up of people who needed or wanted sixty thousand dollars. But let's consider that idea for a bit. The Demarests have sixty thousand dollars. You want it. What are you going to do to get it? If they don't know you, you aim a gun at them and take it. If they do know you, and you therefore feel you have to kill them to keep them quiet, you shoot them down and take it. And you leave them where they fell.

"Now let's explore the matter a little further. Let's say you're afraid, since the number of people who know they had sixty thousand dollars is limited, you might come under suspicion when the bodies are discovered. And if the other suspects have ironclad alibis and yours can't be ironclad, you might even be convicted. So you want to make it appear that the Demarests stole the money themselves. In that case, you'd pack their clothes, cancel their milk delivery, load them into the station wagon and drive them to a pre-dug hole, bury them, drive their car to Staten Island or wherever and abandon it, and let it go at that. But when you buried them, you wouldn't leave George's glasses case and a woman's footprint nearby."

"Not on purpose," Wilks answered, "but the glasses case might have inadvertently been dropped by the murderer just as we thought it had been dropped by George. And the woman's footprint—"

"So it might, except for one thing. If you were going to bury your victims, you'd bury them together. I'd believe theft was the motive if the two bodies had been buried together.

"But when George's body and the suitcases are very carefully buried well below Deirdre's body, I have to say it was because the murderer wanted us, if we were going to find anything, to find her body first. And that puts the glasses case and footprint in a different light. Now it becomes clear that the glasses case wasn't left there to throw suspicion on George. Suspicion would automatically be thrown on George. No, that case was left there for a different reason—to tell us George had done the deed, to spell it out for us so that we wouldn't look for George in that grave. It was to keep us from digging deeper by saying George wasn't there. And the footprint, of course, would be a red herring to give George a reason for killing Deirdre. While he might kill her for playing around, that's questionable. The footprint was to clinch his guilt and again stop us from thinking George might also be dead."

Fellows shrugged. "All right, Sid, now tell me who'd do all this just to steal sixty thousand dollars? Look at the angles this guy has figured. If we never find any bodies, we'll forever think the Demarests stole the money. If we find Deirdre's body, we'll think George did it. And, finally, if we do find George, then we'll think a thief did the job. It was for just this reason that I was convinced a thief hadn't done the job, that that was just another red herring.

"So, as soon as I began to think about it, I was persuaded that we'd be following a wrong track looking for people who needed the money. Instead, I started looking for people who'd

121

like to see the Demarests dead.

"From then on it was a cinch. In the first place, the only people I could come up with who might conceivably like to see George and Deirdre dead were Warren Wilcox and Jerry Somers. Warren had had an affair with Deirdre and who knows what might have happened in there? Also, he had apparently been beaten up by Demarest about it. This is something I didn't think a man who fancies himself as superior to everyone as Wilcox does would like. And Jerry was a prospect, of course, because Deirdre had broken up her marriage and she seemed to hate both the husband she lost and the woman who stole him.

"Then, of course, it was obvious that whoever wanted them dead had wanted this for some time. It was only a matter of waiting for the proper situation to arise. And the sixty thousand dollars represented the proper situation. Thus, that meant the villain had to be one of the group, which left Warren and Jerry again.

"Thirdly, this was an elaborately conceived plan. It was a triple-decker job with three different motives revealed as we peel off the layers and the real motive totally hidden. Could the Fogartys dream up a scheme like that? Could the Randolphs? Could Stanley Somers? Not in a million years. Neither could Jerry Somers. Only from Warren Wilcox, who prides himself on his superior intelligence, could we expect such a plan. And, of course, the grave digging, the carting of bodies and all that couldn't have been done by a woman. She'd have had to have a man's help. It had to be Warren Wilcox. He's the only one I could see who had all the requirements necessary—opportunity, ability, and motive."

Wilks said, "Opportunity, yes. Ability, yes. But I don't quite see motive. Just because George gave him a black eye? Maybe he'd want to pay him back, but how does that involve Deirdre? Remember, he was through with her and having an affair with Jerry Somers. How can you be sure she's not the villain of the piece and got him to help her?"

"That's a good question, Sid, and maybe I'm reaching a little, I don't know, but I do know that I'm sure. Well, for one thing—a recent thing—there's no love lost between Jerry and Warren right now. They're turning on each other, or she's turning on him. You don't really think she'd do that if he could condemn her for murder, do you? Say they're both involved. They'd be tied to each other with chains of blood.

"That's one reason, but there are others. For instance, the original setup leads to the conclusion that George and Deirdre took the money and skipped. The only rational excuse for their doing that would be because George was so hard-pressed for money that this looked like the only way out. But nobody in that group knew what George's financial position was. In fact, he gave the appearance of being pretty well fixed. Warren Wilcox was the only one who thought it was a pose. Warren, the psychiatrist, saw through Demarest's front. Nobody else did. But the man who rigged the murders to look like theft had to be able to guess this motive would stick. Suppose, for example, we investigated and found George was well-heeled. We'd immediately dismiss the idea that he'd stolen the money and look for foul play. Therefore, no one who thought George was well off would have tried to put forth that kind of a motive. And that eliminates everybody except Wilcox right there.

"Then there's Wilcox's dismissal of Deirdre as stupid and worthless, a tramp. There's a bitterness in his manner that doesn't become a man who's tossed over the girl. That kind of man can afford to be generous. This sounds more like the man who's been jilted. Deirdre was not a stupid girl at all. She was a pushover for men but otherwise she was reasonable and intelligent enough. Of all the men in the case, only Wilcox is bitter toward Deirdre. Again that makes him a suspect.

"And then there's that interesting affair Wilcox carried on with Jerry. Its obviousness can hardly have been anything but deliberate. And there's the way it ended—very suddenly—after the pay-offs and murders. Kind of as if it had served its purpose. Everybody had been successfully fooled.

"And if you'll look a little closer, you'll notice that, despite various claims that Wilcox chased women, the only two women there's any real evidence that he chased are Deirdre and Jerry. That's an interesting point in that it has a parallel. Despite what Jerry says about George—all the women he was supposed to chase—the only one there's evidence for is Deirdre. Other character witnesses for George claim he behaved himself up until Deirdre came on the scene. Then there's Stan Somers. He was egged into going after Deirdre and once he started, he kept on. He found he liked it and this broke up his marriage. Deirdre, it appears, had a powerful effect on men. They really went overboard for her."

Wilks frowned. "So you claim Wilcox did likewise?"

"That's my guess. In fact, once you decide Wilcox did the murders, you're forced to that conclusion. Regardless of how it appears on the surface, you have to believe that Wilcox fell hard for Deirdre. He might have proposed marriage, he might have done almost anything. And Deirdre, who was glad to play but happy to remain married to a man who would put up with her infidelities so long as she would stay with him, would find this tedious. My guess has to be that she threw him over, that she got fed up with his jealousies or his seriousness and told him to take off. And when he wouldn't, she got George to back it up with a couple of well-directed punches.

"And Warren, the superior one, would be left feeling inferior to her. And he'd feel inferior to George too. He would have lost caste in front of them and he couldn't stand it. So he'd decide he'd have to re-establish his superiority and prove himself better than they were by killing them. And, to make it stick, outwit the police in the bargain, and to really do justice to his intelligence, compose a most elaborate and intellectually satisfying plot, one that would demonstrate his psychological superiority over everybody. In other words, his plan to get away with murder must not only be successful, it should be beautiful to boot."

28

Warren Wilcox slammed the back door of his home and stood for a moment clutching the box with his manuscript in it and sniffing the cool night air. He had to calm himself but it was very difficult to become calm. Damn Moira. Damn editors, damn the police, damn everybody. His carefully written manuscript that he had lavished so much love and affection on, the sure-fire best seller. It couldn't miss. And now, here it was back home from Doubleday & Company, Inc., rejected. "Disappointing," the accompanying letter called it. "We thought you were writing a book on psychiatry, not Peyton Place on a couch." Stupid editors. Stupid, stupid. Didn't they know what the public wanted? Get it banned in Boston and it was an automatic hit. And his book would get banned in Boston all right. Very well. Doubleday wasn't the only publishing house in the country. Plenty of others would grab it. And meanwhile, he might as well put it to good use again. Back to the office to work on it all evening.

Of course that wasn't where he was going, and of course Moira knew it wasn't. She thought he was going out with another woman. She was sure it was his receptionist. Let her. That was just what he wanted her to think. The trouble was, she didn't seem to care much. She was coldly bitter about it, not the ranting, hysterical Moira he liked to needle. She'd changed over the last few days. Ever since he made the mistake of actually admitting he'd been unfaithful to her. She had changed into a cold, implacable enemy. She'd told that lawyer about George blacking his eye. And if the word got around . . . Damn it, he should never have admitted it. If that chief of police heard about it, him getting ideas about hating instead of robbing. Whoever heard of a police chief reading Freud?

Wilcox got into his car and backed out. Now the fat was really in the fire. He had to turn up a substitute robber before Fellows started turning a spotlight on him. That chief was getting too close for comfort and that wasn't good at all. Of course, no one would ever suspect that he hadn't given Deirdre the brush, that it was she who had done the dismissing.

It made him cringe to think about it. That maddening Deirdre with her way of being willing yet indifferent. You never felt you owned her. You never felt it was just you, that she was even thinking of you. If she never said "no," she never said, "let's." She never made an overture, she never indicated need or desire. That's what made her so provocative. The trouble was trying to analyze it—to analyze yourself. So easy to analyze others. George had married her. And she had let him. Maybe that persuaded George he meant something to her. But how could Warren Wilcox persuade himself? He had wanted to marry her too and she wouldn't listen. He would have divorced Moira for her, left his wife and children, and she couldn't have cared less. And the more he pressed her, the more annoyed she became. That was the mistake. Getting too serious. Until finally she refused to see him any more. Him. Warren Wilcox. Brilliant, capable, loved by his women patients, wealthy, an experienced hand at sex. And he becomes the one man in the world Deirdre refuses to favor.

Then the degrading part. The pleading. The begging. Her cold contempt. And the wrestling with her and ultimately her turning to George to make him stay away. To George who knew. To the one man who really did own her. George had liked hitting him, bruising his face and blackening his eye. Because George didn't really like sharing his wife even if he had to put up with it.

He had to pay them back. He had to show them who was master, who was the really clever one. And he had done that all right. The affair with Jerry to lull them into believing bygones were bygones. The planning. The waiting for some right moment to arrive when he could strike with impunity behind a disguised motive. The careful misleading of the police.

Now that damned Fellows was unwittingly poking close to the truth. Fortunately the means were at hand to divert him but it had taken some fast planning. He'd have to arrange a fall-guy and plant the evidence to convict him. Stan Somers, of course, was it. That abandoned Thunderbird had to be explained and Stan was the only other one who had gone to New York the day after the slaying. Stan would be the choice and Stan would have the money found on him for proof. Good thing he'd buried the money rather than burned it. The satchel might have rotted but the money would be all right. The original idea was for the money to disappear forever but some guardian angel had kept him from destroying it. It would be needed again after all.

And Jerry was going to have to be a fall-guy too. With Stan not living with her any more, there was no way to plant the money where it would point to him. It had to be hidden in Jerry's house, where he had a key and knew the layout. But, since Stan wouldn't have walked out on Jerry and left the money behind, something else had to be improvised. The two of them were in it together. There was that footprint. Planting that had been a lucky inspiration.

And what story would satisfy the police? Stan needed money, obviously. And Fellows wanted that Freud bit satisfied, did he—that the robbers also wanted George and Deirdre dead? But of course. Jerry hated the two of them. She helped put Stan up to it. She would. Hadn't she pushed Stan into Deirdre's bed? She was the type. A manipulator. And Stan went along. And they hid the money in the cellar. As for the falling out, it would be an act, a ruse to hide their complicity. Yes, it would be simple to set up. Get the money from the burial site, enter Jerry's house when she was out, wrap the money in some clothing and hide it in the cellar. Then point the finger and suggest they wouldn't let the money out of their sight. A police search would take care of the rest.

Only one thing. The rifle must never turn up. They might trace it through serial numbers to the store where he bought it and some clerk there might have a long memory.

Warren Wilcox turned off Long Mountain Road onto the scanty trail that led through the now notorious property. He stopped at a familiar tree a good mile from the graves he had dug. It had been a smart move to bury the money so far away. Those cops had combed acres of woods around the graves. It was wise not to underestimate their industry.

He got out of the car and, with a flashlight, made his way in remembered directions a hundred yards through the under-growths. He knew the spot and admired the clever job he had

126

done in disguising it. Not like the grave, which had to look clumsy if it were ever found. This one he had tried to make sure would never be found.

He got down on his knees and started scraping with his hands and then a stick. He had no shovel for that was in George Demarest's garage.

The digging was harder than he expected and his fingers were scratched, his nails broken, when he felt the handle of the satchel. Those hands would have to be back in shape before he saw the police again.

He got the satchel free and dug out the dirt-caked gun. He laid them aside and hurriedly filled in the hole, scattered some leaves, and checked the results with the light of the flash. Satisfied, he gathered his things and started back.

When he opened the passenger door to thrust his treasures in on the floor, a pair of headlights blinked on from a car parked thirty feet back of his. He gasped in shock as he stood caught in the glare, still holding the gun, satchel and flashlight. He didn't really think a couple of neckers were in the car.

Other flashlights came on, pinning him in their beams. From close at hand behind his shoulder he heard Chief Fellows say, "All right, Doctor. We'll take a look at what you've got if you don't mind."

He saw Wilks' face appear in the light a few feet in front of him. He felt the chief take hold of the satchel and rifle and turned helplessly, letting them go. Police were all around him now. It seemed as if there were at least a hundred though he could only count five.

Fellows had the satchel open, examining the contents with a flash. "That's the money," he said in businesslike fashion and handed it to Wilks. He looked at the rifle. "Winchester twenty-two. Model 290. Repeating. It's still got shells in it." He handed that to another policeman and said to Wilcox, "It's my duty to inform you that you have the right to a lawyer. You need not answer any questions—"

NEL BESTSELLERS